P9-EDI-222

Ava could lay down her life for the badge, but she hated the risk to their child.

Harley was right there on the same page with her.

He went to her and took hold of her shoulders. He'd hoped to come up with just the right thing to say to ease some of the tension. But her breath broke, and Ava went into his arms as if she belonged there.

There'd been a time not that long ago when she would have hugged him, and more, but he could tell this was costing her. Because this wasn't out of lust that would lead them straight to bed. This was her leaning on him, and part of her would see that as a weakness.

It wasn't.

Because part of him was leaning on her, too. He needed this, the contact that gave him assurance that the baby and she were alive. Now it was up to both of them to make sure it stayed that way.

MARKED FOR REVENGE

USA TODAY Bestselling Author

DELORES FOSSEN

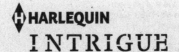

HARLEQUIN
INTRIGUE

If you purchased this book without a cover you should be aware that this book is stolen property. It was reported as "unsold and destroyed" to the publisher, and neither the author nor the publisher has received any payment for this "stripped book."

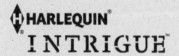

HARLEQUIN®
INTRIGUE™

Recycling programs for this product may not exist in your area.

ISBN-13: 978-1-335-59042-8

Marked for Revenge

Copyright © 2023 by Delores Fossen

All rights reserved. No part of this book may be used or reproduced in any manner whatsoever without written permission except in the case of brief quotations embodied in critical articles and reviews.

This is a work of fiction. Names, characters, places and incidents are either the product of the author's imagination or are used fictitiously. Any resemblance to actual persons, living or dead, businesses, companies, events or locales is entirely coincidental.

For questions and comments about the quality of this book, please contact us at CustomerService@Harlequin.com.

Harlequin Enterprises ULC
22 Adelaide St. West, 41st Floor
Toronto, Ontario M5H 4E3, Canada
www.Harlequin.com

Printed in U.S.A.

Delores Fossen, a *USA TODAY* bestselling author, has written over 150 novels, with millions of copies of her books in print worldwide. She's received a Booksellers' Best Award and an RT Reviewers' Choice Best Book Award. She was also a finalist for a prestigious RITA® Award. You can contact the author through her website at www.deloresfossen.com.

Books by Delores Fossen

Harlequin Intrigue

Silver Creek Lawmen: Second Generation

Targeted in Silver Creek
Maverick Detective Dad
Last Seen in Silver Creek
Marked for Revenge

The Law in Lubbock County

Sheriff in the Saddle
Maverick Justice
Lawman to the Core
Spurred to Justice

Mercy Ridge Lawmen

Her Child to Protect
Safeguarding the Surrogate
Targeting the Deputy
Pursued by the Sheriff

Visit the Author Profile page at Harlequin.com.

CAST OF CHARACTERS

Deputy Ava Lawson—When a serial killer targets her, she must protect her unborn child, even if that means teaming up with her ex, the baby's father.

Texas Ranger Harley Ryland—Shortly after Ava and he split five months ago, she learned she was pregnant. Harley intends not only to be part of his child's life, he'll also do whatever it takes to protect Ava and their baby.

Caleb Franklin—Ava's "secret" son, whom her father forced her to give up when she was a teenager. Now the killer could be using him to get to Ava.

Senator Edgar Lawson—Ava's powerful father doesn't want anyone to know about Caleb and might do anything to keep it secret.

Aaron Walsh—Caleb's biological father and Ava's high school boyfriend. He's had a troubled past and could be killing because of the bad blood between Ava's father and him.

Duran Davidson—Edgar's longtime friend who'd do anything to make sure there are no scandals to hurt Edgar's career and reputation.

Marnie Dunbar—She blames Aaron for her sister's death. Just how far would she go to get back at him?

Chapter One

Deputy Ava Lawson looked down at the dead woman and saw her own face. Not merely a resemblance.

But literally the image of Ava's own face.

Using a photograph of her printed on thin cloth, the killer had molded it to the dead woman.

Ava couldn't stop the slam of emotion and she had to fight just to be able to breathe. Had to fight to stay steady, too, because this kind of stress wouldn't be good for the baby she was carrying. She was in her fifth month, which meant she wasn't at high risk for a miscarriage but she couldn't take the chance of doing harm to this child.

Even though someone else might want exactly that.

Because if she was the target, then so was her precious baby.

"You okay, Ava?" she heard her boss, Sheriff

Theo Sheldon, ask in a murmur. He was standing next to her, taking in the crime scene as she was.

"I'm fine," Ava managed to rasp, both of them knowing it was a lie.

She ran her hand over her stomach and shoved aside the buzzing in her ears. Ava tried to focus on doing her job. Right now, that job included looking for whatever she could find to get some justice for the dead woman.

And the two other dead women who'd come before this one.

Women who'd all been strangled and left posed in the woods around Silver Creek, Texas, Ava's adopted hometown. A town that relied on its sheriff and deputies to protect it from a killer. Right now, law enforcement was failing at that big-time because women were dying.

Ava swept her gaze around the thick cluster of underbrush and trees. It was spring and everything was in bloom. Wildflowers, trees and the shrubs. It was also still cool enough that she wasn't sweating. Not yet anyway.

Thanks to the spotlights the county CSIs had already set up, she didn't have any trouble taking in the scene despite it being night. Since the site was a good two miles from town, this wasn't exactly on the beaten path, but she could see the drag marks that led from the old ranch trail about ten yards away. If the Silver Creek Sheriff's Office hadn't gotten an *anonymous* 9-1-1 call to tell them the location of the body, the dead woman might never have been found. But, of course, the killer had wanted them to know.

Had wanted *Ava* to know.

He'd wanted her to see that image of herself and get the slam of sick dread that came with the realization she was the reason this was happening. And, worse, that she was no closer to stopping this from happening all over again.

Since the first body had turned up three months earlier, Ava, Theo and the other deputies had put in plenty of extra hours at the office. Plenty. They had pored through every crime scene report of the dead women and followed every lead. Ava had also studied all the files of anyone she'd ever arrested, investigated or confronted. Anyone who had popped up on her radar as conceivably connected to a crime.

Because Silver Creek wasn't that big of a town, the number of files and possible persons of interest wasn't exactly staggering, but she had been a deputy for six years now and, before that, a San Antonio cop for eight. Fourteen years in law enforcement meant she'd had ample opportunity to make enemies and rile people, but so far Ava hadn't been able to connect anyone to what was happening now.

The two other victims had been left with the

masks of Ava's face, but there were no other reports of similar crimes in the state. That didn't mean there weren't other murders, though, since the killer could have only started using the masks with these particular victims.

Theo's phone dinged with a text and he muttered some profanity when he read it. "The mayor's heard about the latest murder and he's called in the Texas Rangers."

Ava's head whipped up, her gaze zooming straight to Theo's because she had a bad feeling about this.

"He's called Harley," Theo clarified, showing her the text from the Ranger himself.

Sorry but I've been assigned to your investigation. Will be there soon.

"Good grief," Ava murmured. She didn't need this on top of everything else.

Texas Ranger Harley Ryland. A blast from the past. Both a good and bad one. When she'd been at San Antonio PD, she'd worked with Harley. And had later had a relationship with him, one that had continued as an on-again, off-again kind of deal until five months ago when the off had become permanent.

Things hadn't exactly ended well between them either. Not with Harley being the main reason her scumbag father wasn't in jail. Then, the very day Harley had cleared her dad's name, she'd learned she was pregnant with Harley's child. A child she loved and would raise despite the Texas Ranger being the father. Despite, too, Harley insisting that he would take an active part in parenting the child.

Figuring out how to co-parent with him wouldn't be easy. Ditto for having to work with him again. Along with the tension of being her ex, Harley knew all her past sins and secrets. *All of them*. It was hard to be around someone who had that kind of intimate knowledge about her.

"This is number three," Theo said, drawing her attention back to him—and to the body. "If it's the same guy and not a copycat, we've got a serial killer."

Yes, three was the magic number when it came to earning that particular label. And Ava knew this wasn't a copycat. So did Theo. They hadn't released the specific details of the killer covering the women chin-to-feet with black garbage bags or the cloth photo death masks, and this one appeared to be identical to the other two.

Being careful where she stepped, Ava went closer to watch as the CSI lifted the photo mask from the dead woman's face. Theo cursed again, and Ava knew why. It was because they recognized her.

Monica Howell.

She was a hairdresser at the Sassy Curls Salon just off Main Street. Midthirties, divorced, no kids. But Monica did have parents who lived on a nearby ranch. They were good people and what could be called pillars of the community.

"She wasn't reported missing?" the CSI, Veronica Reyes, asked, looking up at Ava and Theo.

Ava shook her head. If a woman had gone missing anywhere in the tricounty area, the Silver Creek Sheriff's Office would have gotten an alert the moment the report had been filed. That meant Monica's folks, friends and employer hadn't known she'd been taken. That fit, too, with the killer's MO.

The killer didn't keep his victims long. Definitely not long enough to raise any serious red flags about them being missing. From what Theo and she had been able to piece together in the investigation, the other two victims had died less than an hour after they'd last been seen.

"Monica's wearing her work clothes," Theo pointed out when Veronica eased back the black plastic bags from the torso of the body. She was, indeed, since all the salon workers wore powder-blue tops with their names stitched on a breast pocket. "Maybe that means she was grabbed when she was leaving the salon."

"Maybe," Ava agreed, and she mentally went

through the handful of businesses in town that had security cameras. None were anywhere near the salon, but that didn't mean the killer's image hadn't been captured.

Obviously, Theo was on the same page as she was. "I'll have the security camera checked from the traffic light on Main Street," Theo said, stepping away no doubt to call whichever deputy was in the office at this hour. "We might get lucky."

Monica certainly hadn't gotten lucky. She'd been brutalized, murdered and then posed here like garbage. Swallowing hard, fighting back the bile rising in her throat, Ava forced herself to steady when she saw the truck pull to a stop behind the CSIs.

Oh, mercy.

What the heck was he doing here? It was Waylon McClintock, the mayor of Silver Creek, and often a thorn in the side of the sheriff's office. Since Waylon was at the crime scene, Ava figured some thorniness was about to start.

Waylon wasn't alone. Ava silently cursed when she spotted the lanky dark-haired man get out of the passenger's side of Waylon's truck.

Harley.

The CSI lights glinted off the Texas Ranger badge pinned to his shirt as he walked toward her. He was all cowboy cop down to the jeans, cream-colored Stetson and cowboy boots. He was even wearing the traditional crisscross double belt holster that some Rangers favored. It made him look like an Old West gunslinger ready to draw down on the bad guys.

"Deputy," Waylon greeted in his usual gruff tone that always seemed to be a mix of rust and gravel. He glanced over at Theo, who was pacing while he talked on the phone.

"Mayor," Ava greeted back, keeping her own tone hard. She shifted her attention to Harley.

Harley's dark brown eyes met hers, and maybe there was an apology in them. Maybe. But, if so, it was brief because he skimmed his gaze over her baby bump. Just a glance before he turned his attention to the body.

"I heard about the murder from the dispatcher," Waylon snarled. "Woulda been nice to have heard it from Theo or you."

"We've been busy," Ava informed him right back. "We came out as soon as we got the call and have been examining the scene. It's Monica Howell," she added. No way to keep the emotion out of her voice, not with this ripping away at her.

Waylon's sigh was long and he squeezed his eyes shut a moment. "Hell, this is gonna bring her mama and daddy to their knees."

It would, indeed, and Theo and she would be

making the notification as soon as they finished up here.

"I know I don't need to introduce you to Harley," Waylon added with more than a touch of sarcasm as he tipped his head to Harley. "You can't go wrong with the Texas Rangers, especially since you've found squat so far that'll put a stop to these killings. I want these murders to stop. I want the people of my town to feel safe again."

Waylon seemed to be geared up to add more but he hit the pause button when Theo walked back over to them. Theo nodded a greeting to Harley, who was family to him. Not by blood but in every other way. Theo had been raised by former sheriff Grayson Ryland after Theo's parents had been murdered. Grayson's father, Boone, had adopted Harley and his brothers after marrying their mother.

"You could refuse to work with Harley," Waylon went on, talking to both Theo and Ava now, "but why the hell would you? Let him help you fix this problem before you have to tell somebody else's family that their girl's been murdered by a killer you haven't been able to catch."

The guilt didn't just wash over Ava. It slammed through her. Because Waylon was right about them not having caught the killer. And, worse, Ava was positive she was the link to the killer. Not to Waylon, Theo, or to anybody else involved in this investigation. It was her face on those bodies. She was the connection, and Ava had to believe that, sooner or later, the killer would want to end the game he was playing by coming directly after her.

Waylon's phone rang and, when he stepped aside to take the call, Harley turned to Theo. "This is sort of the devil-you-know kind of a situation," Harley explained. "Waylon has connections, and he arranged for a Ranger to be assigned to this. I figured you'd rather me over someone else."

"I would," Theo assured him, but he glanced at Ava, no doubt to see if she agreed.

Of course, Theo knew about her history with Harley. Plenty of gossip in small towns for folks to know she was carrying Harley's baby. Theo also knew that "history" involved her much-despised father. But Ava wouldn't let that history play into this. Wouldn't let the baby or the old heat between Harley and her play into it either. That's why she nodded to let Theo and Harley know she wasn't going to stonewall when it came to getting any help from this particular Ranger.

Harley nodded as well, and turned his attention back to the dead woman. "Tell me about Monica Howell. I went to school with her, but she was a couple of grades behind me so I didn't really know her. She matches the profiles of the other two victims?"

"Monica was divorced and thirty-four," Theo confirmed, reading from the background info he'd pulled up on his phone. "So, yeah, she fits the profile. Female, single or divorced, no kids, in their thirties."

That was also Ava's profile. Well, almost.

"The first victim, Sandy Russo, had several miscarriages," Ava explained, not looking away when Harley's gaze locked with hers. "The second, Theresa Darnell, also had a miscarriage." She had to pause and gather her breath. "When I talk to Monica's parents, I'll ask them if she'd ever been pregnant."

Ava watched as Harley processed that. Others in town might not know about the piece of her life that didn't fit the MO, but he did. During one of their insomnia-night discussions, she'd told him all about her past.

About the child she'd given up for adoption when she was sixteen.

Even now, twenty years later, Ava felt the pain of that. The shame. The anger that it'd been something her father had forced her to do. But that was an old unhealed wound she didn't have time to soothe right now. One that she couldn't use Harley to help her soothe either. They had to stop this killer because the safety of their child was at stake.

"I'm sorry," she heard Harley say under his breath.

Ava wasn't sure if that was a multipronged apology for the murders or for the baggage she'd always carry for giving up her child.

"Your father talked Waylon into calling the Rangers in on this," Harley added a moment later. "I'm sure your dad would have preferred a Ranger other than me, but he definitely pushed Waylon on this."

Everything inside her went still. Not for long though. The fresh wave of anger punched her as hard as the killer had hit Monica. Her father, State Senator Edgar Lawson, didn't live in Silver Creek. Never had. No, his grand estate was over fifty miles away in an exclusive gated neighborhood in San Antonio. That didn't mean, though, that he wouldn't use his power and influence to try to mess around with her life and career.

"Waylon told you this?" she managed to ask.

Harley shook his head. "I have my own contacts, but I found out your father called Waylon and pushed him to bring in outside *assistance*."

Some people might believe her father had done that to help the Silver Creek Sheriff's Office, to make sure his pregnant daughter didn't end up dead in the woods, but Ava knew that Edgar's motives had nothing to do with love. No. He'd have his own reasons, and she would need to find out what those were.

"Your father might not want any bad publicity from having a string of unsolved murders under your jurisdiction," Harley suggested, obviously reading her expression. "After all, he's up for reelection and the press will definitely point out that you're his daughter."

Yes, it could be something as simple as that, and in Edgar's mind, it was bad enough that his heiress daughter was a career cop. Bad enough that she was unmarried and pregnant and wouldn't play the part of being devoted to him so as to help him keep his seat in the Texas senate. But *bad* would be multiplied many times over when the media continued to point out that the senator's daughter hadn't been able to stop a killer who was terrorizing the town where she was a deputy.

A killer who had to be connected to her since the snake was covering the dead women's faces with her photo.

"We have a problem," she heard Veronica call out. The CSI got up and practically ran away from the body.

"What's wrong?" Theo and Harley asked in unison.

"We need to evacuate the scene and get a bomb squad out here right now," Veronica blurted. "There's a bomb beneath the body."

Chapter Two

When Harley had gone to the latest crime scene, he hadn't expected to be chased out of the area because of a bomb. But that's exactly what'd happened. Ava, he and the rest of the responders had been forced to evacuate and hope like hell that they didn't get killed in an explosion the killer had set up.

Harley had had the additional fear of Ava and the baby being hurt. Thankfully, though, they'd all gotten safely out of there so the bomb squad could be called in to do their job. Then Harley had gotten on with doing his.

For starters, Harley knew he really needed to take a harder look at the area where the killer had dumped this latest body. He also needed to find some evidence and find it fast because he wasn't sure how much time they had before the killer struck again.

Correction—how much time Ava had.

A thought that tightened every muscle in his body.

Because Ava was pregnant, it meant she didn't precisely fit the profile of the other murdered women, but it was obvious the killer had "involved her" by using her face on the masks. Maybe the fact Ava was pregnant didn't play into this sick plan. Or the pregnancy could be at the core of it. It was something he needed to try to work out and fast.

And that's exactly what Harley was trying to do now.

Sipping coffee that was strong and bitter enough to burn a hole in his stomach, Harley sat in the chair next to Ava's desk in the Silver Creek Sheriff's Office and waited for Ava and Theo to return. A wait he wasn't sure how long would last, but he was using the time to study the files on the previous two murders.

Harley practically had the entire building to himself tonight since Waylon thankfully hadn't accompanied him to the sheriff's office. No reason for it. Waylon had already gotten what was no doubt his cheap thrill for the night by reminding Theo, and Ava, that he had plenty of power in town. Not that his power was ever in dispute. He had it. Money, too. And apparently the man had enough allies to keep his butt firmly planted in the mayor's seat.

Harley glanced up when the phone rang and he halfway listened when Deputy Diana Warner took the call. Other than Harley, she was the sole occupant of the building, and was working Dispatch and doing what appeared to be a mountain of paperwork. The other deputies were no doubt out in the field, trying to track down any leads on the killer.

The call seemed to be about some cattle breaking fence and getting on the road, so Harley tuned it out and went back to the files. And to waiting.

After Theo and Ava had been told it could be hours before a bomb squad showed up and cleared the explosive, Ava and Theo had left to drive to Monica's parents to tell them of their daughter's murder. Neither Ava nor Theo had invited him to go along with them, and Harley hadn't pressed. Ava already had enough blows to handle tonight without him adding more, even though he would have liked to get in a question or two with the dead woman's parents. That way, he might be able to figure out why the killer had left explosives under her body.

There'd certainly been no other such devices near the other two dead women, and it was always a flashing red light when a murderer changed his MO. Of course, maybe the killer was still evolving, still creating a signature that some predators had. The MO was a given in a crime, but not every serial killer had a signature.

This one did though.

The facial beatings, posing the bodies, the locations of the dumpsites, drugging the victims. And, of course, the cloth masks. The ones of Ava's face.

Yeah, this killer had a very sick signature.

Harley suspected that seeing those masks was giving Ava some nightmares. But that was just the tip of the iceberg. She was a veteran cop. A good one. And she had to know that, one way or another, this executioner had her in his sights. That twisted at Harley, too, because he doubted the killer would give any consideration to the fact that Ava was pregnant.

In fact, the pregnancy might be a motive for the murders.

No way could he ignore the fact that the murders had started three months ago, right about the time Ava was letting people, including Harley, know she was pregnant. So far, this sick SOB had seemingly gone after women who'd lost babies, and maybe that's what the killer wanted in store for Ava. Harley had to make damn sure that didn't happen.

Because Ava had shared the ultrasound results with him, he knew she was carrying a girl. A daughter. Before Ava had told him she was pregnant, Harley had never actually considered fatherhood, but he was more than considering it now. He wanted his baby girl in his life, wanted to be the best possible father he could be, and that started with keeping Ava and her safe.

He glanced up from his laptop again when the front door opened. Since he was sitting in the open-bay bullpen, Harley had no trouble spotting Ava and Theo as they came in. He also had no trouble spotting just how much of a toll the notification had taken. They looked weary and exhausted.

"I need to call the bomb squad and push for some answers on what the heck is going on," Theo said to him, "but Ava can go ahead and update you on what we do have." He headed into his office.

"How rough was the notification?" Harley asked.

Ava nodded and sank down in her desk chair. "Rough." She squeezed her eyes shut a moment. "I really need to stop this guy."

Yeah, and he figured some of that need was because the crimes were personal in that they were linked to Ava. Unfortunately, Harley had read nothing in the case files to indicate what exactly that link was.

"Monica had a miscarriage when she was married," Ava added a moment later.

"So, that fits with the other victims." He waited until her gaze came back to his and then leaned in and lowered his voice to a whisper. "How many people know you had a child when you were a teenager?"

Her mouth tightened a little. "Only a handful who are still living. You, my father, the baby's father and Duran Davidson."

No need for her to spell out that Duran was her father's close friend along with being his campaign manager. Harley suspected Duran had done all sorts of things for his boss. Maybe even covered up a crime or two.

Ava sighed. "I gave birth to the baby in Dallas under an alias that my father had set up, but the housekeepers might have overheard something. If there was gossip, though, it didn't get back to me."

It was possible Edgar had paid off the staff to stay quiet. But money didn't always buy silence. After all these years, someone could have spilled Ava's secret.

"How long were you in Dallas before the baby was born?" Harley asked, hoping it would spur her to aim her thoughts in that direction. It wasn't necessarily the right direction though. The murders could be connected to something much more recent in Ava's life, like her pregnancy, but it was ground that needed to be covered.

"Four and a half months," Ava answered. "Before I started showing, my father arranged for me to stay with Duran's grandparents, who owned a ranch outside Dallas. Then he told everyone I was doing a student exchange program in Ireland for six months. The grandparents died years ago, and they would have never gone against my father. They kept quiet about my pregnancy and the baby."

Maybe, but all it would take was one slip of the tongue and people would know the senator had a pregnant teenage daughter. Still, Harley couldn't see how such a slip would come back to the murders. If Ava was the key, and he was positive she was, then there had to be a trigger that'd gotten all of this started.

"How about the baby's father?" Harley pressed, still keeping his voice low so the deputy wouldn't overhear. "Would he have told someone?"

She took a moment, obviously processing that. "It's possible. I haven't seen or heard from him since my father whisked me away in secret to Dallas, but his name is Aaron Walsh." Ava paused again. "After the first murder, I ran a background check on him." She typed in something on her laptop, pulled up a file, and turned the screen so he could read it.

It only took a glance for Harley to see that Aaron Walsh hadn't exactly led a charmed life. Orphaned at a young age and brought up in foster care, he was two years older than Ava, which meant he would have been eighteen when she got pregnant.

During that "too much to drink" confession, Ava had said her father had threatened Aaron with jail time to force her into giving up the baby for adoption. Her father had also used that jail time threat to basically run Aaron out of San Antonio and force the young man's silence. But since the statute of limitations would have played into this at the seven-year point, how had Edgar made sure that Ava's lover would stay quiet?

That was a question he'd ask Edgar, and Harley didn't think the man was going to like having the past tossed in his face.

Harley kept reading from the background check on Aaron. Shortly after Aaron had left San Antonio, he'd done a six-month stint in jail for auto theft. He'd stayed clean behind bars and had gotten an early release. After that, he'd done two more years on parole. And that was it. Nothing else in the background.

"I haven't been able to find anything else on Aaron," Ava explained. "He didn't put in for a legal name change, but it's possible he moved and just started using an alias. Or he could have stolen the identity he's using."

Yeah. Harley mentally played with that for a couple of moments. Maybe the jail time and experience with Ava's father had left Aaron bitter enough to disappear.

Or to kill.

"If it is Aaron who's doing this, why wait twenty years to start killing?" Harley muttered, hoping that by saying it aloud, a good theory would come to him. But he came up with nothing.

Ava shook her head. "I told Theo about my former boyfriends, including Aaron. I didn't tell him about the baby," she quickly added. "But I briefed Theo on anyone from my past who could play into this." She paused. "Now, I need to tell him that I had a child. Until tonight, I wasn't sure a pregnancy or baby was part of the profile. I mean the others had had miscarriages, but I never did."

Harley picked up on that thread. "You were thinking more along the lines of someone tormenting you because you'd failed to get justice or had gotten justice that was a trigger for the killer to go after you?"

"Yes. And that might still be what this is. I don't want to dismiss it in case the killer is using my face on those masks as some kind of diversion to throw us off his scent." She paused. Probably had to, because all of this was no doubt hitting her hard. "But with the third victim having had a miscarriage, there's a strong possibility that it's connected."

Harley made a sound of agreement but didn't add more because Deputy Diana Warner walked past them, heading to Theo's office with some call memos.

"Any reason you didn't run for sheriff when my uncle Grayson retired?" Harley asked Ava while he glanced around the bullpen. Better to switch to a less personal topic with Diana in hearing range. "You're the most experienced deputy."

"Because I dislike paperwork and politics." Ava shrugged. "Plus, Theo's a lot better as sheriff than I'd ever be."

Harley figured that was true about Theo, who had a way of soothing ruffled feathers while still staying in control of a situation. Theo was born to be a cop, and so was Ava. Ironic, since she was practically Texas royalty. Four generations of state senators, congressmen, judges, etcetera. Four generations of old money that had added even more money to the family coffers. Harley figured her ancestors were shaking their heads over why she'd want to ditch all of that and pin on a badge.

She opened her mouth to say something else but obviously rethought it when Diana returned from Theo's office and passed by them again. "You'll be staying with your folks at the family ranch?" she asked him instead.

Harley nodded, though the term *family ranch*

wasn't an adequate description. It was more of a sprawling estate with an equally sprawling ranch and multiple homes for the three generations of the still-growing Ryland clan. Many of his siblings and cousins lived there.

"Mom's baking and Dad wants us to go fishing," Harley added to the conversation. He probably wouldn't have time for a fishing trip, but he needed to carve out a few hours with his folks. His adoptive dad, Boone, was in his eighties now, so Harley needed to make more of an effort to be with him and his mom.

Theo was finishing up a phone call when he finally came out of his office and made a beeline toward them while slipping his phone into the pocket of his jeans. "The bomb wasn't active. It was the real deal with enough explosives to take out anyone within ten feet of the body, but there was no timer or switch to detonate it."

"So why put it there?" Harley had to ask.

Theo shook his head and, in a weary gesture, he scrubbed his hand over his face. "Maybe just to add another layer of fear."

Maybe. The killer was definitely playing games with them. "The Ranger lab might be able to find out if the bomb has a signature." A long shot, especially considering the killer hadn't used such a device before. Still, he'd either made it himself or gotten it from someone who could have left a signature with other bombs.

"Mind if we go into your office?" Ava asked Theo. "There's something I need to tell you."

Theo stared at her a moment before shifting his gaze to Harley. Then he nodded and motioned for them to follow him. However, they'd only made it a few steps before the front door flew open and the visitors stormed in.

The operative words being *flew* and *stormed*.

Senator Edgar Lawson entered, followed by Duran Davidson, and they brought with them an urgency that seemed to radiate off them in thick, hot waves.

"Ava," Edgar immediately said. There was plenty of concern in his voice, but Harley wasn't sure how genuine it was.

Edgar was one of those people who had a powerful presence just by coming into a room. That was in part because of his size. He was six-foot-four. And, even though he was in his sixties, he still sported the body that had earned him plenty of accolades back in the day when he'd been a college football star. He modeled the good-ol'-boy looks, too, which he no doubt kept fresh with the occasional plastic surgery that made him look a good decade younger.

Duran was a different story and had a presence of a totally different kind. Lanky to the point of being bony, with sharp features and ink-black hair that only emphasized his too-pale skin. His movements were jerky, clumsy and he always seemed to be on the verge of tripping over his own feet. Or apologizing. Harley had discovered the man was good at that. Placating, apologizing, groveling or doing whatever it took to keep his boss in a favorable limelight.

Harley didn't trust either of them one little bit.

And, despite Duran's wimpy demeanor, Harley suspected the man was capable of just about anything. He'd have to be to have stayed this close to Edgar for all this time.

Edgar slid his gaze over them and scowled when his attention landed on Ava's stomach. Publicly, Edgar had played up the fact that he'd soon be a grandfather, but Harley figured the man despised him for getting Ava pregnant. Worse, Edgar couldn't shove Harley out of the picture the way he had Aaron. That almost certainly overrode Edgar's feelings of gratitude over Harley's part in keeping him out of jail. If the man had such feelings, that is. Edgar might have dismissed it as Harley simply doing his job.

"I heard about the latest murder," Edgar said, aiming his comment not at Ava or Theo but at Harley. "And I want to know what the heck you're doing about it. My daughter is obviously in danger."

"Your daughter is a cop who can take care of herself," Ava snarled, and she added a huff to that. "We're in the middle of an investigation, so unless you have pertinent info, you need to leave."

Well, that took care of Edgar's concerned look. His eyes didn't narrow. His jaw didn't go stiff. But Harley detected some anger simmering behind that oily façade.

"As a matter of fact, I do have something," Edgar said, matching his daughter's tone with one that was just a tad too sappy-sweet. He motioned toward Duran, who handed a thick manila envelope to Harley. Or rather, he tried to do that. Harley didn't take it.

Instead, Harley hitched his thumb to Theo. "He's the sheriff and the one in charge of this investigation."

Oh, that didn't set well with Edgar, and Harley added a checkmark on his mental chart of ways to rile the senator. Yeah, it was petty, but Harley didn't like being played, and he was certain that's what Edgar was doing now. And what he'd actually done with the investigation where Harley had been forced to clear the man's name.

Edgar gave Duran a subtle nod, which must have been a green light because he handed Theo the envelope. "Those are copies of the senator's threat files. The more recent ones," he clarified when Theo made a show of looking at the thickness of the envelope.

"I shouldn't have to tell you to keep those private," Edgar interjected. "No need to give mean, ugly people any more attention than they deserve. I just wanted you to have it in case it connects in some way to the murders."

"Why would you think the killer would have any connection to you?" Harley asked.

Edgar opened his mouth, closed it and obviously rethought what he'd been about to say. "I know about the masks the sick bastard puts on the victims. I know it's my daughter's face."

Ava groaned, and Harley muttered some profanity under his breath.

"That info wasn't released to the public," Theo quickly pointed out.

"I'm not the public," Edgar fired back. "If the murders are linked to Ava, then they could be linked to me, linked to something in those files," he added, tipping his head to the envelope. "Somebody might be trying to cause trouble for me and the campaign by creating havoc in the county that Ava has decided to call home."

"Do you have someone specific in mind?" Theo asked. "A political adversary? A riled lover?"

"I don't have a riled lover," Edgar quickly

noted, "and my opponent probably wouldn't go to such lengths."

Harley would check on both of those possibilities, but he already had some info on the "lover" part. When he'd been spearheading the investigation that'd dealt with Edgar possibly being involved in black-market land sales, Harley had had to interview Valerie Chandler, the widowed socialite who'd been Edgar's companion for going on two decades. Edgar had started appearing in public with the woman several years after Ava's mother had been killed in a car accident when Ava had been just eight.

"This is costing Edgar votes," Duran piped in. "With each murder, he's taken a dip in the polls."

Ava groaned and threw her hands up in the air. "Pardon me if I'm more worried about three women being dead more than I am poll rankings."

"I'm worried, too. Worried about you and my grandchild. About me," Edgar admitted. "About the election. Do something to find this killer and stop him," he snarled while he volleyed glances to Harley and Theo. Not to Ava though. He obviously didn't have a lot of faith in his daughter's cop skills.

Theo's phone rang and he muttered, "I have to take this," when he looked at the screen. Tucking the envelope under his arm, he went to his office.

Edgar, and therefore Duran, turned to leave, but Harley stepped in front of them. "When's the last time you heard from Aaron Walsh?" Harley asked, keeping his voice low since Diana was back at the dispatch desk.

Now, Edgar's eyes narrowed and he aimed a strong shot of venom at Ava. "You told him?"

"I did," she readily confirmed, stepping to Harley's side. "Answer the question."

Edgar kept up the steely glare for several snail-crawling moments before he finally snarled, "I haven't seen or spoken to that worthless piece of trash in twenty years. But I have kept tabs on him."

"Tabs?" Harley and Ava questioned in unison.

"I have a PI assigned to keep an eye on him, to make sure he doesn't try to worm his way back into my daughter's life."

Ava exchanged a glance with Harley before she said anything. "So, you know where Aaron is?" she asked her father.

"I did. He was living in Bulverde, using the name Eddie Walker, until about seven months ago. His live-in girlfriend died of an overdose and he disappeared. The PI hasn't been able to find him since, though he's had reports that Aaron is still in the Bulverde area."

Harley huffed. "And you didn't think it was

relevant to tell someone this? Bulverde is only a thirty-minute drive from Silver Creek."

"No, it wasn't relevant," Edgar snapped. "That man doesn't have anything to do…" He stopped and obviously clued in to why Aaron's where-abouts would be important.

"We'll want any and all info you have on Aaron Walsh," Ava insisted.

That brought on a fresh glare from her father. "Any and all info that'll remain private."

She shook her head. "I can't guarantee that. If Aaron is a killer, his history with me will have to come out."

It was the truth, but it was fuel to an already hot fire, and Edgar looked ready to explode. Duran must have thought so, too, because he nudged Edgar and tipped his head to Diana, a reminder to his boss that this conversation could be overheard.

The fit of temper stayed in Edgar's eyes, but he did lower his voice and aim his index finger at Harley. "I pushed to get the Rangers brought in on this. I can push to have you removed from this investigation."

Harley looked the man straight in the eye. "Go ahead, push. See where it gets you. I'm on this investigation whether in an official capacity or not. And I won't obstruct justice by concealing evidence that might save lives. It might save your butt in the polls, too," he reminded the man.

Apparently, Edgar decided he couldn't argue with that. Or rather, that he didn't intend to verbally argue anyway. Maybe that was because of Diana's presence or because Theo was making his way back toward them.

"This isn't over," Edgar murmured like a threat as the two men went out with the same speed and intensity as they'd entered.

Harley was about to explain what had caused the pair's hasty exit, but then he looked at Theo's expression. Oh, hell. What now?

"Once the bomb was removed," Theo said, starting that with a heavy sigh, "the CSIs found a note beneath it." He lifted his phone screen for them to see.

Harley repeated that "Oh, hell," but this time it was aloud. Ava didn't say anything. She merely stared at the screen. At the words written on the note.

This is all for you, Mom.

Chapter Three

Ava's throat clamped shut and she couldn't breathe. Couldn't move. Couldn't speak. She just stood there and felt the words stab out at her.

This is all for you, Mom.

"In my office, now," Theo insisted. Not in a demand-for-answers sort of way but rather with mountains of concern. That was probably because she looked ready to drop to the floor.

Harley hooked his arm around her waist to steady her and to get her moving. Good thing, too, since she wasn't sure she could have managed to take a single step on her own.

Oh, God.

Was the child she'd given birth to all those years ago actually responsible for this? Ava's mind wouldn't process the answer.

Theo shut the door once they were in his office and went to the fridge to get her a bottle of water while Harley helped her to a chair. She nearly asked Harley to fill Theo in on what the note meant, but Ava forced herself to steel up. She was a deputy, for heaven's sake, and she could do this. She gulped down some water and looked up at her boss.

"When I was sixteen, I had a baby. A boy," she managed to add, "and I gave him up for adoption."

"Edgar forced her to do that," Harley supplied. "And he also forced her to keep the pregnancy a secret."

Dragging in a long breath, Theo sank down into his chair, putting himself at eye level with her. "That means the child would be nineteen or twenty now?"

"Twenty," she confirmed. Twenty years, two months and four days.

She could have given him the hour had it been necessary.

Ava paused again, drank some more water and continued. "It was a closed, private adoption, but after I became a cop, I managed to get hold of the records." And she hoped Theo didn't ask how she'd managed that. "He was adopted by Megan and Gene Franklin, both teachers, from Kerrville. They got him when he was two days old, and they named him Caleb James."

It was the first time Ava had allowed herself to say his name out loud. Her son's name. Except he wasn't hers. Never had been because she'd never even been allowed to hold him. Per her father's orders, the baby had been whisked away from her only seconds after he'd drawn his first breath.

"I should point out that Caleb probably isn't the actual killer," Harley said. "If he was doing this, why point a huge neon arrow at himself?"

Ava latched onto that like a lifeline. The note was basically a confession—if Caleb was the killer, that is. But if he'd wanted to confess, why not just come to the source? To her. So, this meant someone had set him up, had wanted her to believe that Caleb might be killing because of her.

"You've met Caleb and the Franklins?" Theo asked, drawing her attention back to him.

She shook her head. "No, but I've seen a couple of pictures of them on social media. Not many, but I recall a few years back, they celebrated their thirtieth wedding anniversary. Caleb's a criminal justice major at University of Texas."

That was in Austin, less than an hour from Silver Creek, where the murdered women had been dumped.

That caused Ava to groan. Cops looked at means, motive and opportunity when it came to identifying a criminal. The opportunity could have been there since Caleb lived so close, and the person who'd set him up would know that.

Except there was something else. Something Ava didn't want to consider but had to.

That Caleb had used the note as a way to make them believe he was innocent.

A sort of reverse psychology. One that would involve him in the investigation where he might have an easier time getting to her. So he could kill her.

"Is Caleb's bio father in the picture?" Theo pressed.

"Not if he listened to my father's threats, he isn't." Ava didn't bother mincing words that might have painted Edgar in a better light. "His name is Aaron Walsh, but he's apparently been using the name Eddie Walker. My father threatened him with jail time if he didn't disappear, so that's what he did. I just learned my father has had a PI keeping an eye on him. We should have the PI records soon." If not, she'd have a *conversation* with her dad.

"I'll go ahead and order a background check on him and the alias," Theo said, shifting his attention to his laptop. While he typed in the request, Ava gave him Aaron's birthdate and the address where he'd lived when they'd dated.

"If Aaron was run out of town," Theo went on after he'd finished the request, "it's possible he's holding a grudge. Maybe against Edgar. Maybe against you, too," he added to Ava.

Harley made a sound of agreement. "And according to Edgar, Aaron's girlfriend died of an overdose about a year ago. That could be the trigger that got him to start planning and executing the murders."

The icy chill went through Ava, skin to bone. It was something she should have considered right off—and she probably would have had the note not put an F-5 tornado in her head.

"All right, we'll locate Aaron and bring him in for questioning," Theo continued. "Give me the names of anyone else who knew that you'd had a child."

"Harley and I were going over that when we were in the bullpen," Ava said. "The only living people are my father, Duran, Harley, me and now you. The couple I lived with when I was pregnant have both passed away. So has the doctor who delivered the baby."

"Passed away of natural causes?" Theo asked, obviously latching right onto the possibility of foul play.

"Yes. I checked," Ava assured him. She glanced at Harley. "Because I know my father is capable of pretty much anything and can't be trusted."

Harley didn't wince, didn't dodge her gaze, either, but he had to know she'd just sent a zing his way. "I agree with you," he readily admitted. "But Edgar was set up for those black-market land deals, and I had no choice but to drop the investigation."

Theo turned to Harley. "I remember you mentioning that. It happened...when, about six months ago?"

"Five months," Harley verified. Since Theo knew that Ava was five months pregnant and the baby was Harley's, he could no doubt figure out why Ava and he had split.

And that was something else Ava had yet to consider. Even though it was a bitter pill to swallow, she had to accept that her father had undeniably been innocent and framed, and that meant there was someone out there who wanted to ruin Edgar. Maybe it had escalated into the murders because going after her could be a way to get back at Edgar.

"I can check my father's alibis for the times of the murders," she suggested. "Because if it is someone trying again to set him up, we could use the alibis to establish his innocence. If we make that public, it could stop someone else from being killed."

Of course, that was a long shot, but it was something they needed to at least consider. A big problem, though, would be getting her father to agree to it. He likely wouldn't want it known that he was possibly the reason these murders were happening.

"At my father's insistence, I used an alias when I was pregnant and delivered the baby," Ava continued. "There are medical records under that name Alyssa Monroe. I don't think there's anything in them, though, that could link back to me, but we should take a closer look just in case."

Theo nodded and jotted down the name. "Have you gotten any messages or threats over the years that have to do with the child you gave up?"

"No." She didn't have to search her memory for that particular answer. If someone had contacted her about Caleb or Aaron, she would have remembered.

Another nod from Theo. This time, he leaned back in his chair. "What do you think Caleb would have done if he'd found out he's adopted and you're his birth mother? A birth mother who's now pregnant and intends on keeping her child?"

This time, she had to pause, and then she shook her head. "I don't have a clue because I don't know him. I don't know his adoptive parents, either, and don't have any idea how they'd react if they knew a senator's daughter had given birth to their son."

But it was definitely something to think about, and Ava had already gotten started on that thinking when her phone dinged. It was a short text from Duran.

"The PI just emailed the sheriff the info on Aaron Walsh," Ava relayed.

Ava immediately showed the text to Harley and Theo, and Theo went to his emails while Harley and she positioned themselves behind him so they could see the laptop screen. When Theo opened the file, she was shocked to see that it was over a thousand pages of reports.

"Well," Theo muttered, "this surveillance has obviously been going on a while."

It had been indeed and had started the same week Aaron had left San Antonio, and Ava. Theo quickly scanned through the years until he got to the most recent ones where Aaron had been living in Bulverde as Eddie Walker.

There was an attached coroner's report of his girlfriend's death that Ava would want to take a look at later but, for now, they focused on the PI's latest attempts to find Aaron. The PI had highlighted the name and phone number of the dead girlfriend's sister, Marnie Dunbar, who also lived in Bulverde, and he had added a note that he was certain Marnie knew Aaron's whereabouts.

Ava checked the time. It was close to midnight, late to be making a call, but she didn't want to wait until morning. Obviously, Theo thought so as well, because he took out his phone, pressed in the number and put the call on speaker. It took four rings, but someone finally answered.

"Yeah?" the woman said, sounding very groggy. No surprise there. She'd probably been asleep.

"I'm Sheriff Theo Sheldon," Theo greeted, "and I'm sorry to bother you. Are you Marnie Dunbar?"

"Yeah," she repeated. "Why are you asking?"

"I'm trying to track down Aaron Walsh, aka Eddie Walker."

There was a groan followed by a huff. "What do you want with him?" Marnie snapped. The grogginess was gone and Ava knew defensiveness when she heard it. What Ava didn't hear was any kind of surprise over Aaron using an alias.

"I just need to talk to him," Theo assured her. "Do you have a contact number, or can you tell me how to reach him?"

"No, I can't—"

"I'm a friend of Aaron's," Ava interrupted because she knew the woman was within a fraction of a second of ending the call. "It's important we talk to him because he could be in danger," she lied.

Well, maybe it was a lie. They didn't know how, or if, Aaron fit into the picture.

"Danger how, why?" The woman was no longer defensive or riled, but she didn't seem overly worried either.

"I'm sorry, but I can't give you the specifics of an active investigation," Ava insisted. "We just need to find him and make sure he's okay."

There was a long silence. "You're really his friend?" she asked.

"I was. I'm Ava Lawson. Maybe you heard him mention me."

"No, I don't think so. How do you know him?"

Ava decided to go with a piece of the truth. "We went to school together. He was my boyfriend."

Another silence. "You're the rich girl he dated."

"Yes," Ava answered after a pause of her own. "He mentioned me?"

"He told Christina—that's my sister—that he'd gotten messed up over some rich girl back in high school. I'm guessing you two had a bad breakup or something?"

"Or something," Ava muttered. It didn't surprise her that Aaron had gotten "messed up" over her. Or more specifically, over their situation of her being pregnant with his child. She had certainly been in the messed-up category, too. "How is Aaron?"

"He's a train wreck right now. Correction, he's been a train wreck since I've known him. In fact, I don't have a whole lot of love for the SOB, and

I think Christina would still be alive if she hadn't gotten mixed up with him."

"Oh?" Ava settled for saying, hoping it would spur the woman to continue. It did.

"Yeah, Christina wanted to marry him and start a family."

That caused Ava's breath to stall a little and she braced herself in case Christina was about to admit that Aaron had confessed to her that he had a child. But she didn't.

"My sister just couldn't see the bad in him," Marnie added.

"What kind of bad?" Ava pressed. "Drugs?"

Marnie groaned. Then cursed. "He didn't use drugs, not that I know of. He used my sister. He'd go off drinking with his friends and wouldn't come back for days. When she would get mad, he'd try to put it all on her, telling her if she'd quit nagging him, he wouldn't have to drink." She paused. "But I will say when Christina died, it just about ripped him to pieces. He fell apart at the funeral."

Maybe it'd done enough *ripping* to set Aaron on the path to murder.

"Christina had a drug problem?" Ava asked, hoping to get more insight into what had gone on.

"No." Marnie paused, cursed, then groaned. "Okay, so she used every now and then, but she got a bad batch or something, and it caused her heart to stop. Aaron was at work and didn't find her for hours."

"I'm sorry," Ava said and hoped it didn't sound too abrupt to move on to the next question. "What kind of work does Aaron do these days?"

"He's a mechanic," the woman readily answered. "A decent one from what I hear. When he's sober, he can build just about anything."

Ava wondered if that included a bomb. Yes, she really needed to have a chat with Aaron all right.

"You said Aaron might be in some kind of danger?" Marnie continued a moment later. "Is that because of Christina's death?"

"Maybe," Ava settled for saying. "We're looking into some possibilities. Was anyone arrested for supplying the drugs to your sister?"

"No. We don't know who she bought them from. Aaron asked around, of course, but if he ever got a name, he didn't tell me." She made a grumbling sound. "You don't think the drug dealer is after him, do you?"

Ava went with a safe answer that would hopefully get the woman to cooperate. "Like I said, we're looking into that possibility. Do you have his number so I can talk to him about it?"

Marnie groaned again, and Ava could practically see the woman biting her lip while she mentally debated what to do. "Even though he didn't always treat my sister right, she loved him, and I wouldn't feel right just giving you his number what with you being a cop and all. But I'll call him and let him know you're looking for him. You said your name was Ava Larson?"

"Lawson," Ava corrected. "Take down my number," she added and waited for Marnie to give her the go-ahead to do that before rattling it off. Then, Ava tried to imagine how Aaron would react when he learned she was looking for him. "Tell him it's about what happened when he was eighteen," she added.

Maybe that would stir Aaron's curiosity enough for him to call her. Of course, if he was the killer, he might be waiting for contact like this. Might even welcome it.

"I will," Marnie assured her and paused again. "If he really is in some kind of danger, you intend to make sure he stays safe?"

"We'll try," she said and ended the call. Again, it was a lie because if Aaron was the killer, keeping him safe was the last thing Ava intended. However, she would make sure he was locked up so he couldn't hurt or kill anyone else.

It was hard for her to wrap her mind around the fact that her high school boyfriend, who'd been her first lover, was now a down and broken man. Then again, her father had had a good start on breaking Aaron so maybe that was playing into this. Payback that would strike out at her father and her, and Aaron might consider the other dead women collateral damage.

"I'll record the conversation if Aaron calls me," Ava told Harley and Theo. "In the meantime, maybe we can get someone to Bulverde to press Marnie on his whereabouts."

"The Rangers can handle that," Harley said. "I can get someone from the San Antonio office to go to her place."

"Do it," Theo said with a nod, and he waited for Harley to send a text before he turned back to Ava.

She saw the not-so-subtle shift of emotion in Theo's eyes. There was worry and concern, and Ava knew it was for her.

For what he was about to tell her.

"Get some rest," Theo instructed. "Both of you," he added to Harley. "You'll be staying with Ava tonight?"

Ava was about to nix that, but then it occurred to her that if Aaron or Caleb was behind these murders, then she was definitely in danger. That meant so was the baby. She didn't especially want Harley as an overnight guest, but she also didn't want to take any unnecessary risks. Not having readily available backup would definitely be a risk.

Harley looked at her, no doubt waiting to see if

she was going to issue him an invitation to stay with her. She sighed then nodded.

"Good," Theo said. "Get some sleep. Then, first thing in the morning, we'll drive into San Antonio." He looked Ava straight in the eyes. "I want Harley and you with me when I interview your son."

Chapter Four

Harley knew he was on shaky ground by going to Ava's house with her, but, thankfully, she hadn't protested. Well, she hadn't with words anyway, though he could see the disapproval in every inch of her body language.

Hell, he'd disapprove, too, if he were in her shoes. But Ava was a smart cop and she understood the bottom line here.

Their child was in danger.

It didn't matter that Ava and he weren't on the best of terms. Didn't matter, either, that those terms might stay bad. Both of them loved their unborn baby and would do whatever was necessary to keep her safe.

While Ava drove them from the sheriff's office to her house, Harley focused on the list that Duran had sent them. Possible candidates for those wanting to use Ava to get back at Edgar. Harley didn't think the killer's name would be listed there, but since it was a possibility, it had to be checked.

"I might be able to get through that faster than you since it's possible I'm already familiar with some of the names," Ava commented, glancing over at him. Glancing, too, at the road, as Harley was doing. Both of them were keeping watch of their surroundings to make sure they weren't about to be attacked.

"I'll half it with you," Harley offered after he gave it some thought. "Ditto for halving the list we'll no doubt get from the bomb squad once they have a signature of who could have made that bomb."

"Yes," she murmured, and he heard the other emotions snaking beneath that one-word response. That's because she was no doubt thinking of what had been on that note beneath the bomb.

This is all for you, Mom.

Without Ava's picture on the masks, Harley could have reasoned that the killer was going after women he was punishing for something his mother had done or hadn't done. But that mask either meant Ava was the mom figure in this scenario or else that's what the killer wanted them to believe.

That meant...well, anything.

Because if the killer was only using Ava to

throw them off his scent, then the murders could be about anything, including any and all connections to anyone in Silver Creek. Or to her father. Or, hell, to anyone else for that matter.

Harley wasn't able to bite back the grumbled profanity over the frustration that they had three dead women and no answers that would get them closer to stopping this sick SOB before he went after someone else.

Ava turned into the driveway of her house and Harley was glad to see the security lights flare on as her vehicle approached. He knew, too, that she had a good security system that would have alerted her had anyone tried to break in. Still, systems could and did fail, so they couldn't let down their guard.

She used the remote on her visor to open the garage door and neither of them got out until the door closed behind them. Neither actually removed their guns from their holsters, but they placed their hands over them.

Ava stepped in first, with Harley right behind her, and they immediately went in to start a search of the place. Harley had been here before so he knew his way around, and he headed for the hall where the bedrooms were located. He searched the guest room, the master and the two bathrooms before he made it to the nursery. The crib was already in place, giving him a jab of emotion. And worry. Soon, Ava and he would be parents, and he figured some worries would still be there. But he didn't want a serial killer to be on their list of concerns.

After he was sure there were no signs of a break-in or an intruder, Harley made his way back into the main part of the house to join Ava, who was at the sink taking some meds. No, not actual meds, he realized when he saw the bottle, but rather a prenatal vitamin.

Harley certainly hadn't needed another reminder of the baby, but he got a couple what with the vitamin and the chalkboard wall next to the fridge. There were names on it.

Abigail, Rebecca, Gracelyn, Holly, Laine, Isabel, Jemma, Carly.

"I jot down possible baby names as they come to mind," she explained when she followed his eyes. "I'd planned on asking you for input," Ava added.

"Thanks for that," he said. Harley picked up the chalk from the ledge above the board and added two names. Olivia and Charlotte.

Ava nodded her approval and tipped her head to the hall. "You can use the guest room," she said, all business now. She was no doubt making sure he remembered there was a reason he was being sent there and not to her own bed.

She looked at him, and Harley felt the old

punch of heat when their gazes connected. Old but still somehow new and fresh. Apparently, his body had no intentions of letting him forget that Ava had once been his lover, even if he wouldn't be sharing her bed.

"Go ahead and send me my half of the names from Duran," she said, pulling her eyes from his. "I'll look them over before I fall asleep."

Harley frowned because he figured if she was looking over possible candidates for a serial killer, then she wouldn't be getting much sleep. "Let's just both glance through them now. *Glance*," he emphasized. "And then you can get some sleep."

Her silence let him know she was debating that, but Ava finally motioned for him to follow her to her office. She booted up her laptop and opened the file after Harley sent it to her from his phone.

"Hundreds of them," she muttered on a sigh.

Harley had done some sighing as well, and he pointed out the names that Duran or Edgar had highlighted. "Those are the people who tried to set up your father for the black-market land deals that were basically fronts for money laundering."

It was a sore subject, all right. Because it'd been this very investigation that had caused her to break off things with Harley.

Ava's mouth tightened. "You've already investigated these people." It wasn't a question, and there was a chill in her voice to go along with that tightness.

"I have," he confirmed. "I found offshore accounts and false documents to prove they had indeed set him up."

"You found what my father wanted you to find," she muttered. "That doesn't mean he was innocent."

"No," Harley agreed, and then he stared at her until she made eye contact with him again. "Are you ever going to be able to forgive me for dropping the charges against him?"

"No," Ava snapped, but then she sighed again and waved that off. "I don't want to get into all of this again."

Part of him didn't want to push her on this. Not when she was tired and had been through hell and back over the past couple of hours. But another part of him wanted to give it one last shot at trying to clear the air between them.

"I had a strong gut feeling that Edgar had some kind of connection to those land deals. Maybe connections he wasn't aware of at the start, but when the investigation started, I believe he covered his tracks so all the evidence would point to them." He tapped the names that had been highlighted. "Trust me when I say that I looked for anything and everything that could prove your father's involvement."

She shifted her attention from him and back to the list, but her body language was still defensive and all business. "Could any of the men on that list have committed these murders to get back at my father?"

He sighed, and while he wished they'd been able to dive into the more personal parts of this situation, Ava did have a valid question. "No," he assured her. "They're all in jail and are being monitored closely for any attempts at retaliation."

"*Closely monitored* doesn't mean they couldn't find a way," she quickly pointed out.

Harley made an equally quick sound of agreement. "True, but I don't think they'd do that because I also believe your father might have paid them to take the fall for him. They won't spend that much time in jail, and your father could have made sure they were well compensated for their silence."

That got her attention and Ava's gaze speared right to his. "Is there any proof of that?"

"None," he said.

What he didn't add was that he was still digging, still looking for any connection whatsoever that his gut feeling was right. And that gut feeling was that Edgar was a dangerous criminal. Unfortunately, Harley couldn't see how murdering three women and linking those murders to his daughter would earn him anything.

Unless…

"Just how mad was your father when he found out you were carrying my baby?" Harley asked.

"Mad," she answered while she studied him. He saw the exact moment she realized where Harley was going with this. "You think Edgar's so enraged that he plans to murder me and make it look as if it's a serial killer's doing." She shook her head. "Then, why drag Caleb into it by leaving that Mom note?"

Harley hadn't thought that far into this possible theory, but he instantly made a connection. A bad one. "What if Edgar's worried that the way he handled your teen pregnancy will come to light? He won't come out looking good in the eyes of the voters. After all, he forced his daughter into giving up her child and threatened her boyfriend with jail time."

Her forehead bunched up while she obviously gave that some thought. "It's possible Edgar's worried about that," she finally conceded. "But that would mean something has happened to make him believe that what he did is about to come out."

"Secrets get uncovered all the time," Harley pointed out. Even though it was a stretch for him to believe that Edgar would want his own daughter dead because of an ugly secret being revealed. Then again, Edgar wasn't a loving, devoted father, and he might be willing to go to any lengths to prevent himself from being dragged into a scandal.

"If this is about getting revenge by killing me," Ava said, "or wanting to cover up what he did all those years ago, then Edgar wouldn't want anything to be made public about Caleb."

"True." Harley had to give it some thought as well. "This theory might be out there, but maybe Edgar intends for Caleb to be blamed."

He was about to expand that theory when his phone dinged with a text. Since it was from Theo, Harley figured the sheriff hadn't taken his own advice about getting some rest.

Harley froze when he read the single sentence Theo had sent. Froze and then cursed. "Caleb's adoptive parents were both killed in a car crash seven months ago."

Judging from the way Ava sucked in her breath, she hadn't had a clue. But she certainly knew what it could mean. Losing one's parents was traumatic and it could have triggered some kind of break.

Ava groaned and would have no doubt tried to wrap her mind around that, but her phone rang. Considering how late it was, he figured this wouldn't be good news, and his stomach automatically knotted. He hoped like hell there hadn't been another murder.

"It's Marnie," Ava relayed to him. "I added her info to my contacts because I'd given her my number," she explained while she took the call and put it on speaker.

"Ava Lawson?" the woman immediately asked. There was an urgency in her voice.

"Yes, it's me. Marnie, how can I help you?"

Despite that urgency, Marnie didn't jump to answer. "This might be nothing, but after we talked, I got to thinking about Aaron. About the last time I saw him. It wasn't long after Christina died, and he came over to drop off some of Christina's clothes and personal items that he thought I might want. He was drunk and rambling, so I'm not even sure what he said was important."

"What did he say?" Now, Ava was doling out some of her own urgency.

"Remember, he was rambling," Marnie reminded her, "and he was going on about talking to somebody who was connected to some things that happened to him when he was a teenager. After your call where you told me you were once involved with him, I wondered if Aaron was talking about you."

Harley wanted to jump in with a bunch of questions. Specifically questions that might connect anything Aaron had said to the murders, but he held back because he figured Ava would be able to get more from the woman without him interrupting.

"Did Aaron give you any details about what happened to him?" Ava prompted. "And did he say who the person was and why he was talking to him or her?"

"Sort of. He talked about being scared, that he had to stay quiet about something or that he could be in big trouble. I thought he maybe meant Christina's drug dealer, but Aaron kept going on and on about being a teenager and making a mistake. A mistake he said that'd come back to haunt him because now he was being threatened."

"'Threatened,'" Ava repeated in a murmur. She cleared her throat before she asked, "Did Aaron mention the name of the person who was threatening him?"

Harley automatically moved closer to the phone, wondering if the woman was about to tell them it was Ava's father.

But it wasn't Edgar's name that came out of Marnie's mouth.

"Caleb," Marnie said. "I'm pretty sure that's who Aaron kept going on about. Aaron was really worried that this Caleb was going to do something to hurt him."

Chapter Five

One of the things that Ava missed most with her pregnancy was not being able to have enough coffee to clear her head. And, right now, while Harley was driving them to Austin, she could have used a serious amount of caffeine to do just that.

She'd barely slept, and that was in part due to having Harley just up the hall from her. Also in part because the images of all three of the murder victims had continued to flash in her head like grisly neon signs. But Caleb's name had done some flashing, too, and the thought of him being connected to all of this put ice in her blood.

Mercy, she prayed he was innocent.

Marnie's claim of what she'd heard Aaron say would have to be investigated, of course, and questions about that would be included in the interview that would soon be starting.

According to the call Ava had just gotten from Theo, he was already in Austin since he'd wanted to stop by the local PD there to let them know he was on their turf. The plan was for Theo to then meet Harley and her for the interview. Because there had been concerns that Caleb might flee, Theo hadn't told him that two Silver Creek cops and a Texas Ranger would soon be arriving on his doorstep. But Caleb was supposedly at his apartment near the campus because the Rangers had set up surveillance on him to make sure he stayed put.

And that he didn't slip off to kill anyone.

"My offer still stands," Harley said, yanking her out of her thoughts. "Theo and I can do this interview, record it, and you can listen to it later."

It was tempting if only so she could avoid the stress this might put on the baby, but Ava had to know the truth. She didn't want to learn that truth from a recording. If the son she'd given up for adoption wanted her dead and was killing in her name, she needed to face him and deal with it.

"Thanks, but I'm doing this," she stated. "And I do mean the thanks," she added so he'd understand that she appreciated it.

Right now, she'd take all the help she could get. She was in danger, which meant so was her baby and anyone around her, and that danger could be connected to her father. Or her son. But Ava was hoping it was neither of them, that this was just the killer's attempts to make it look connected.

She hated her father, but if he was indeed the one killing women and targeting her, then it was going to create an emotional nightmare. Still, if Edgar had anything to do with this, she wanted him punished and punished hard.

Harley pulled Ava's car to a stop in front of the Crossroads Apartments. Not upscale but not a dump either. Since it was only a few blocks from campus, she was betting most of the residents were students.

"Have you changed your mind about not telling Caleb who you are?" Harley asked.

She shook her head. "I want to see his reaction to me. If he knows I'm his birth mother, I might see some signs of recognition even if he doesn't volunteer it. If he doesn't know, then that's an indication he's innocent in all of this."

Harley made a sound of agreement and gave her a look that let her know he was worried about her going through this. So was she, but that wouldn't stop her.

Ava took some deep breaths, trying to steel herself up as they got out of the car. She automatically glanced around, looking for any signs of trouble. No trouble, but she spotted Theo already outside the door to Caleb's apartment.

"That's the Ranger who's been watching the place," Harley informed her, tipping his head to the gray Ford Focus on the far side of the parking lot. He waved to the Ranger who then drove away now that he knew Theo had backup. "If we decide to keep eyes on Caleb after we finish, then I can have him come back."

She was hoping that wouldn't be necessary, that with just this interview, they'd be able to eliminate Caleb as a suspect and be absolutely certain he was innocent.

Theo, too, studied Ava's expression when they got closer to him, and he must have been satisfied she could handle whatever was about to happen because he rang the doorbell. Ava had to tamp down another slam of nerves when she heard the footsteps.

"He has a roommate, Jonah Chavez, but he's not home," Theo explained, keeping his voice low. "According to the Ranger, the roommate left about an hour ago."

Good, because Ava thought it would be even harder if this interview played out in front of someone else. Then again, it was possible once Caleb realized they were there to talk to him about a trio of murders, he might want a lawyer present.

The door opened and the young man looked out at them with both surprise and caution in his eyes. Eyes that were a genetic copy of Ava's. That was the first thing she noticed about him, and she didn't have to look hard to see the resemblance to Aaron, either, with his sandy-blond hair and square jaw. Aaron had been handsome as a teenager, and he'd obviously passed those genes along to Caleb.

"Yes?" Caleb said, his attention landing first on Theo. Then Theo's badge. "Is something wrong? Did something happen to one of my friends?" Now, there was alarm in the young man's eyes and he shifted his gaze to Harley. Then to Ava.

And there she saw it.

The recognition that she wished hadn't been there. Caleb knew who she was. He knew, and that meant he'd just zoomed to the top of their suspect list.

"Your friends are all fine as far as we know," Theo said. "I'm Sheriff Theo Sheldon." He tipped his head toward Harley and her. "This is Texas Ranger Harley Ryland and Deputy Ava Lawson."

"Yes," Caleb muttered, his eyes locked with hers. He stayed like that, staring at her, until he finally gave his head a little shake as if to clear it. He stepped back, motioning for them to come in.

But not before his attention landed on her baby bump.

Ava hated that he immediately turned to move out of the doorway because it meant she couldn't see his reaction. In the couple of seconds that it took him to get into the living area, he could have managed to compose himself. Well, he could have if he was very good at concealing what was going on in his head.

They stepped inside, automatically glancing around to take in the place. Since it was small, there wasn't much to take in, and even the doors to the two bedrooms were both open. Ava saw no weapons and, thankfully, no sick "shrines" to her that would indicate she was the motive for murder.

"Wow," Caleb said, still staring at her. "I didn't expect this. I mean, I thought I might meet you one day, but I always figured it'd be just the two of us. And that I'd be better prepared for it," he added with a nervous chuckle.

Ava found herself latching onto every word. As both a mom and a cop. And she studied his face for signs of resentment or calculation. She didn't see any, but she had to accept that might be because she didn't want to see it. That's why she was thankful Harley and Theo were with her. They would be able to see anything that didn't make it through her mental blinders.

"How did you find out who I am?" Ava asked. She had plenty of questions but decided to go with that one first.

"Oh…" he started but then held up his finger in a wait-a-second gesture.

He went to the adjoining kitchen, which, of

course, put them all on alert in case this was a ploy to grab a weapon, but Caleb simply poured himself a glass of water and downed most of it.

"All right," Caleb said, coming back toward them. He repeated those two words as if to steady himself, but there were still plenty of nerves showing when he finally continued.

"After I lost my parents in a car wreck, I was a mess and thought having answers about my bio-parents would help, so I did one of those DNA tests," he explained. "It came back with some genetic cousins. I sorted through them until I saw that many of them were connected to the surname Walsh. I emailed some of them, asking if anyone knew who my bio-parents were, and one cousin said my bio-dad might be Aaron Walsh but that the family had lost touch with him."

Ava felt everything inside her go still. Even with all Edgar's wrangling to keep the pregnancy a secret, Caleb had unraveled the truth with a DNA test and some digging. Again, she had to fight the urge to fire off a bunch of questions. Questions that might alarm Caleb and have him withholding information. Right now, it was best if she just stayed quiet and let him finish.

"No one seemed to know where Aaron Walsh was," he went on. "My roommate's mom is a PI, so as a favor, she looked into finding him. It took more than a month, but she was finally able to track him down. She got his phone number and I called him. When I told him who I was and when I was born, he said yeah, that I was probably his son."

There was no stillness in the reaction Ava had to that. Her heart dropped and her chest tightened. It shouldn't have shocked her that a private investigator could get this kind of info since Edgar's PI had managed it, but still she hadn't expected Aaron to confirm that he was possibly Caleb's father. Not after the threats Edgar had doled out to Aaron.

"Aaron told me if he was actually my bio-dad then you'd be my bio-mom," Caleb explained. "So, that sent me back to the DNA cousins and, sure enough, I found a couple of your distant relatives. None of them took my calls or answered my emails, but I figured that's because I was somewhat of a family secret."

Oh, yes. Edgar had made sure of that, and part of Ava was glad that her father hadn't been able to keep all of it buried. But there were some possible big problems with the truth coming out. For instance, had her father known about any of this and then set a murder plan in motion?

"How long ago did you have that conversation with Aaron?" Harley asked. And Ava knew the reason for the question. Harley was trying to pin down if learning about his bio-parents had been around the time the murders had started.

Caleb didn't even have to pause to give it some thought. "Four months ago. I remember the exact date because it was the five-month anniversary of my parents' deaths."

Oh, mercy. The first murder had happened three months ago, so the timing could fit since the killer would have needed a while to work out the details of the murders. Caleb seemed awfully calm and collected for a serial killer who was now facing three badges, but Ava couldn't use that to dismiss him as a suspect.

"Look," Caleb continued, "my parents were awesome, and they always told me up-front that I was adopted. Because the adoption records were sealed, they didn't know any info about my bios. I just thought it would help with my grief, that's all." His gaze met Ava's. "And I never intended to interfere with your life. Or Aaron's."

He seemed so sincere and, heaven help her, she believed every word he was saying. Later, she'd find out if Harley and Theo did, too.

"What exactly did Aaron tell you about me and him?" Ava asked.

"Not a whole lot, and FYI, I asked him if he wanted to meet me and he said sure, but then he wouldn't come up with a time or a place. I got the idea that he was still dealing with some bad things because of me."

"Not because of you," Ava quickly corrected. No way did she want to put blame for what had happened on Caleb's shoulders. "You know who my father is?" she tacked on.

Caleb gave a slow nod. "Aaron didn't have anything good to say about him."

Ava didn't spell out that was because there wasn't much good to say about Edgar. "I got pregnant with you when I was sixteen, and my father took many steps to ensure it was kept secret."

Oh, how much to say Ava didn't want to come off sounding as if none of what had happened had been her fault. After all, she hadn't taken proper precautions and had gotten pregnant.

If she'd been stronger, she could have run away, had the baby and kept him. But even then, as a teenager, Ava had known that would have ended up being a tough life for her baby since she'd had no way to support him. Added to that, she'd known her father would have carried through on his threat and made sure Aaron ended up in jail.

Considering what Marnie had told them, maybe Edgar was still trying to make that happen.

"Yeah, Aaron said he didn't see you after you

told him you were pregnant, and he figured your dad had hidden you some place. Aaron said he looked for you but couldn't find you."

That was probably true. She had looked for him as well, all the while knowing they could never be together. That had crushed her back then, but considering the kind of man Aaron had become, she figured a relationship wouldn't have worked out between them. Especially with her father doing everything to destroy Aaron.

"Aaron and I wanted to keep you, but we couldn't," Ava settled for saying, and she braced herself, figuring that Caleb would lash out at her for not doing more.

A lashing she would absolutely deserve.

He didn't. His body language tightened some, suggesting he was still trying to come to terms with his feelings about her and what she'd done, but there was no venom or anger.

"You're pregnant," Caleb murmured, his gaze dropping to her stomach.

She nodded and automatically brushed her hand over her stomach, her gaze pinned to Caleb to try to gauge his reaction. "I'm in my fifth month."

It was hard to tell, but she thought that maybe he hadn't known before today. Of course, she hadn't posted about it on social media, and she wasn't in the media's eye enough for them to pick up on it.

Not yet anyway.

If the murders continued and if the bit about the masks leaked, she had no doubts that she would soon be the center of a media firestorm.

Caleb shifted his attention to Harley and Theo, his eyes looking down at their hands, maybe to try to spot a wedding ring. There weren't any, though Theo was engaged to the Silver Creek assistant district attorney, Kim Ryland.

"I'm guessing the three of you didn't come here just to talk about Deputy Lawson being my birth mom," Caleb remarked. "What's wrong? Is Aaron in some kind of trouble?"

Ava shook her head and then shrugged because she had no idea if Aaron truly was in trouble. Maybe he was, but for now she had to focus on the main reason for this visit.

"Three women have been murdered in or around Silver Creek in the past three months," she stated, trying to keep all the emotion out of her voice. She wouldn't mention the masks since that tidbit was being withheld from the public. "The murders seem to be connected to me."

Caleb's shoulders snapped back. "Connected how?" he asked.

"The killer left a note at the last crime scene," Harley answered. "We haven't identified the killer, but we know he's somehow linked to Deputy Lawson and that he could be killing to get back at her in some way."

Caleb shook his head as if puzzled by that, and then his eyes went wide. "You think I killed somebody. I didn't," he quickly added. He staggered back a step, his pleading gaze going to Ava. "You have to believe me. I wouldn't kill anybody."

"Are you angry about her giving you up for adoption?" Harley pressed.

"No." His reply was fast and loud. "I mean, I guess I wondered why she didn't want to keep me, but then Aaron told me they were just teenagers, so I understood. And, hell, even if I was angry, I still wouldn't kill anyone."

"I'm going to go ahead and Mirandize you." Theo spoke up, causing the color to drain from Caleb's face. "It's for your protection, so you know your rights," he added.

Caleb didn't make a sound while Theo gave him the Miranda warning, but he did sink down onto the sofa and put his face in his hands for a moment.

"Do you want a lawyer present?" Theo asked him once he'd finished.

Caleb looked at her, maybe trying to decide if he could trust her not to allow him to be railroaded. He must have decided he could because he shook his head. "I've done nothing wrong, so go ahead and ask me whatever it is you came here for."

Theo took out a piece of paper and handed it to Caleb. "Where were you on those dates and at those hours?"

Caleb dragged in some quick breaths, but then he seemed to steady himself when he actually looked at the paper. "Yes. For this one anyway." He tapped the first date. "I was at a weekend seminar in Dallas. I didn't post about it on social media because my roommate was with me for that, and I didn't want to let anyone know the apartment would be empty."

Theo nodded and handed Caleb a small notepad he took from his pocket. "Jot down the name of the seminar and the person in charge of it. What about the other two dates?" Theo prompted after Caleb had finished writing.

Caleb took out his phone and pulled up his calendar. Some of the color came back to his cheeks. "I was with someone on the third date." He looked up at Theo. "I'll give you her name and contact info, but when you talk to her, don't make it sound like I'm some kind of killer. I'm not, and I really like her. I don't want this to screw things up between us."

"I won't volunteer any details, and I'll make it

seem routine. I've found if I throw in the words *background check*, most people just accept that."

Caleb sighed in a way that could be interpreted that he hoped it was true and then shook his head. "I don't have anything on my calendar for this second one. It was right before a big exam, and I was here studying. My roommate spent that night at his folks since it was some kind of family deal. Does this mean you'll arrest me?"

"No," Theo informed him. "I'll look into the other two alibis, and if they check out, then I can ask around and see if anyone saw you on the other night in question." He paused a heartbeat. "Ever had any experience with explosives?"

Again, Caleb's eyes widened. "No. Well, nothing other than cherry bombs on the Fourth of July, but that doesn't count. Right?" he questioned, his demeanor more than a little shaky.

"It doesn't count," Theo assured him. "But I will ask around and find out if you've been lying to me."

"I haven't been," Caleb quickly insisted and then shifted his attention back to Ava. "How are the murders connected to you? Are you in danger?"

No way could Ava spill any other details about the killings, but she could answer the second part. Well, sort of answer it anyway. "Maybe I'm in danger. Can you think of anyone who'd want to set you up so we'd think you had a part in the murders?"

"No." Again, his answer was quick and his face was a textbook picture of shock. He slowly got to his feet. "No," he repeated. "I mean there are some people who might not like me, but there's not enough hate to kill."

As a cop, Ava knew it didn't always take a lot of hate. Murders happened with all levels of heat, and these particular murders felt cold to her. Calculated and organized. Certainly, they hadn't been done in the heat of anger.

Theo tipped his head to the notepad Caleb was still holding. "Write down the names of those who don't like you. Include any you might have broken up with or rejected in some kind of way."

This was standard procedure but, like Ava, Theo knew it probably wouldn't help them come up with the names of suspects. Besides, they already had names.

Her father, Duran and Aaron.

And the next step would be to question all three of them, along with pressing her father and Duran to find out if one of them was still threatening Aaron.

Caleb handed Theo the notepad after he was finished, and Theo looked it over. The sheriff was no doubt doing a mental comparison to the handwriting on the note that'd been left at the last crime scene. Ava had a look, too, but she couldn't see a resemblance. Still, Theo would have it analyzed.

"I really don't want to mess up anything in your life," Caleb said, looking at her now. "But I'm glad I got to meet you." He opened his mouth, but he must have changed his mind as to whatever he'd been about to say because he shook his head and waved it off.

"I'm glad I got to meet you, too," she said once she managed to clear the lump in her throat.

Their gazes stayed connected with the silence hanging between them, and then Caleb looked away. "Am I in danger?" he asked, not aiming that at anyone in particular. "I mean, if this killer is trying to set me up, maybe he'll come after me."

No way could any of them dismiss the possibility, and hearing it spelled out tightened her chest so much that it was hard for her to breathe. She was ready to offer private protection, a bodyguard, but Harley spoke first.

"I'll have the Texas Rangers keep an eye on you, and you'll need to take some precautions. For instance, don't go anywhere alone at night and be aware of your surroundings. If you see or sense anyone watching or following you, call me, the sheriff or Deputy Lawson."

Harley handed Caleb a business card with his contact info, and Ava and Theo did the same.

"Thanks," Caleb muttered.

Ava could tell he was scared and, along with tightening her chest even more, it riled her to the core that someone was doing this to him.

To her son.

Yes, she allowed the thought in her head. Someone was playing sick games with her son and her, and she had to figure out a way to make it stop. Even if this was the one and only time she got to see the child she'd delivered all those years ago, she wanted him safe.

And she loved him.

That was the other emotion that came through loud and clear. Maybe it was some kind of primal DNA connection, a survival of the species thing, but she loved him.

"Call us if you think of anything else," Ava reminded Caleb, hoping that was an invitation for him to contact her. That contact probably wouldn't be easy, but part of her wanted it more than her next breath.

Rather than risk saying anything she shouldn't, Ava turned to go to the door. Theo and Harley were right behind her.

"Thanks for your cooperation," Theo told Caleb. "One of us will be in touch with you soon."

They stepped outside and Harley immediately took out his phone. "I'll get the Ranger back out here. We can wait in the car until he shows."

"Good," Theo confirmed. "I'll get started on checking these alibis as soon as I'm back in Silver Creek." With that, Theo headed to his cruiser and Harley and Ava went toward her car.

They didn't get far.

Gunfire cracked through the air.

Chapter Six

Harley reacted out of training and instinct when he heard the gunshot. He hooked his arm around Ava and pulled her to the ground, having her land on top of him so the fall wouldn't be so jarring.

He instantly thought of their baby. Of the child Ava would want him to protect at all costs, and even though she was a cop, he had to make sure she was all right.

Before he could move in front of Ava to shield her, there was the sound of another gunshot. This bullet slammed into the vehicle they were using for cover.

Terrified that the shot had ricocheted and hit Ava, he glanced back at her. She wasn't bleeding, thank God, and while she had her gun drawn, she also had her arm over her stomach. Protecting the baby even though all hell was breaking loose around them.

"Theo," Ava blurted. "Is he okay?"

Harley couldn't see him without lifting his

head, and at the moment that wouldn't be a good idea. However, he hoped like the devil that the sheriff had managed to either get inside his cruiser or was close enough he wouldn't be out in the open and an easy target.

A third shot came, slamming into the car's windshield, and it told Harley loads. The shooter was positioned across the street, probably on the roof of the two-story apartment building that faced Caleb's door. The shooter also didn't have the best aim or he would have already succeeded in hitting them.

Not exactly a comforting thought.

Ditto for the realization that either Ava or he was the target since so far all the shots had come directly at them. But Harley could be certain of something else. Caleb wasn't the shooter. No way could he have gotten out of his apartment and across the street in the couple of minutes since they'd left him.

"Stay down," he heard Theo shout.

Just as there was another round of gunfire. Maybe folks would listen because this was a situation where there could be some collateral damage.

"I've called the Austin cops," someone shouted. Caleb.

Because Ava's left arm was against his back,

Harley felt her tense, and she muttered some profanity. "Caleb, stay down!" she called out to him.

She didn't add anything else. Didn't have to. Harley had seen the emotion in her eyes as she'd looked at him when they'd been in his apartment. Even if she didn't want to have deep feelings of love for her son, she did. It was already there, and love could be a bad distraction. Harley had firsthand knowledge of that because he loved his unborn child, and here this SOB shooter was putting her in danger.

Harley adjusted his position just a little so he could get a better look at the building across the street. He couldn't see the shooter or the barrel of a rifle—the weapon the guy must be using to get this kind of range. Harley also couldn't see any side stairs, thus he wouldn't be able to get a glimpse of the shooter if he tried to come down from the roof. It was possible there were stairs at the back, but since it was only two floors, he could have used whatever fire escape was available.

In the distance, he heard the wail of the sirens. It wouldn't be long before the local cops arrived. Thank God. Every second Ava was out here was a second that he could lose her and the baby.

Harley braced himself for more shots. And, even though he probably wouldn't be able to return fire in the middle of the city, he wanted to have his gun ready in case this snake threw all caution to the wind and came down those steps firing on all cylinders.

But Harley doubted that was the plan.

No, if this was their killer, it didn't fit with his MO. He was a snatch-and-grab kind of attacker. One who liked to play sick mind games with Ava. So, maybe that's what this was all about. It could explain why the shots had missed them. If so, the killer was no doubt already hurrying for cover to plan his next move.

Harley glanced in the direction of a cruiser as it stopped just up the street. The cops inside were likely checking to see if this was a scenario with active fire. Harley figured Theo was in contact with them about just that, and they were working out how to respond.

Some movement caught Harley's eye. Not on the stairs or the roof but at the right side of the building where the shots had originated. It was a tall, lanky man with sandy-blond hair, and while he didn't appear to be armed, he was looking in their direction.

"You see him?" Ava muttered, motioning just as the man took off running. He wasn't coming toward them but away from the apartment where the shots had been fired.

Harley nodded and kept his gaze pinned to him. At least he did until he heard Ava gasp.

Harley snapped his attention toward her, praying that she hadn't just realized she'd been shot. But she wasn't looking at any part of her body. Her focus, too, was on the man.

"I know him," she said, her breath rushing out with her words. "That's Aaron Walsh."

WHILE THE EMT checked her blood pressure, Ava tried to level her breathing and settle her nerves. Hard to do, considering that someone had just tried to kill Harley and her. But she had to at least try to calm down for the sake of the baby. And so she could have a clear enough head to help the Austin cops in any way.

They had to find Aaron.

Ava was certain that had been Aaron fleeing the scene and, thankfully, the cops had been able to respond by going after him in pursuit. A pursuit still underway while Harley and she were at police headquarters. Theo had whisked them there in his bullet-resistant cruiser since it was the station nearest the shooting and, after they'd all given brief statements, the sheriff had left to assist in the search for Aaron.

Before Theo had done that, though, he'd insisted Ava stay put and be checked out by the EMTs who were already en route to do the exam at the police station. Ava hadn't refused. Despite her not having any visible injuries, she needed the baby checked, and Harley had done more insisting by letting her know that he'd be staying with her. Maybe in part to make sure she remained in place, but she also knew he was as worried about their daughter as she was.

Caleb was okay, and that helped big-time with her raw nerves. Because Caleb had had her phone number, he'd texted her several times to ask how she was doing and to let her know that he hadn't been hurt. In fact, there'd been no reported injuries, which was somewhat of a miracle, considering multiple shots had been fired into a heavily populated area.

Ava's phone dinged again with another text, but this time it wasn't from Caleb. It was from her father, so she ignored it. She'd already declined two calls from him so it was obvious he was trying to find another way to get her to communicate. Since Edgar worked in Austin when the senate was in session, Ava wouldn't put it past either of the men to try to find her location and come see her. After all, it wouldn't do for the senator not to personally respond to an attack on his daughter.

"Are you cramping or having any contractions?" the EMT asked, yanking Ava's attention back to the exam. According to her name tag, she was Lisa Mendoza.

Ava shook her head.

"What about spotting?" the EMT pressed, prompting Ava to shake her head again. "And has the baby moved since the incident?"

"Yes," Ava verified. "She's moving now."

"Good," the EMT said. "I need you to lift your top so I can listen to the baby's heartbeat with this fetal Doppler." She took the device from the medical supply bag.

Ava was wearing a loose shirt to cover her bump, but she hesitated when she started to lift it. It was foolish, of course, since Harley had seen her naked. Ditto for her seeing him naked as well. However, it occurred to her that he'd yet to see her baby bump. He had gone with her to some of her appointments, but he'd always looked away whenever it required her to bare any part of her body.

That's what Harley did now, too.

"It's okay," Ava told him. Why, she didn't know, but after what they'd just been through, it seemed ridiculous that he wouldn't be able to see that particular part of her. Especially since he was clearly waiting on pins and needles to make sure the baby was okay.

"Ranger Ryland is the baby's father," Ava explained to the EMT when the woman hesitated.

Ava lifted her top and pulled down the waist of her maternity jeans, and the EMT got the wand in place. "How far along are you?" she asked, and she kept her attention on the Doppler monitor she was holding in her left hand.

"Twenty weeks. Halfway there," she added in a murmur though she was certain Harley was already aware of that.

Moments later, the EMT smiled. "The baby's heartbeat is strong." She continued to move the wand around. "And steady." She showed the monitor to both of them. The average was a hundred and forty beats per minute, which Ava knew was normal.

Some of the tightness in Ava's chest finally eased. Thank heavens her baby was all right.

"Everything looks good," the EMT said, packing her things away. "I'd advise you to go ahead and make an appointment for a check with your regular OB."

Ava nodded because she'd expected that. Obviously, Harley hadn't because that put some fresh alarm on his face.

"It's routine," Ava assured him.

The EMT made a sound of agreement and stood. "Anytime the mother has experienced any kind of trauma, we advise her to speak with her doctor. You're sure you don't want me to give you a quick checkup?" she tacked onto that, glancing at Harley.

He'd declined the EMT's first offer and he nixed the idea again. "I'm not hurt."

Ava doubted that was true. There was blood on the knee of his jeans. He'd likely scraped it when he'd gotten her behind the cover of that car. Later, she'd remind him to at least check it himself and make sure it didn't need a bandage.

"Thank you," Ava muttered to him after the EMT left them in the office that one of the lieutenants, Scott O'Malley, had allowed them to use.

"For what?" he asked.

"For getting me and the baby out of the line of fire."

He shrugged, but there was nothing casual about the gesture. No. This had hit him as hard as it'd hit her, which meant they'd both be dealing with it for a long time. Worse, it might not be over.

She stood so she could give her jeans an adjustment, and Harley turned to her just as she looked up at him. Their gazes connected. Held. And they both muttered some profanity. No need for her to question why he was cursing. He didn't want this heat any more than she did. Because the timing sucked. Now wasn't the time to try to work out any personal stuff between them. Not when they had to focus on stopping a killer.

"Why do you think the killer came after us like this?" she asked. "Why break his MO?" And then she threw in a possible answer. "Is it because he thought Caleb might be able to tell us something that would ID him?"

Ava watched Harley's expression, looking for any signs that he was going to say that Caleb did this to throw him off his scent. But Harley probably wouldn't go there. If Caleb was indeed the killer and wanted to cover his tracks, he wouldn't have left the Mom note with the third body.

"Possibly," Harley said a moment later. "Or it could have been a warning. Keep coming after him, and we'll pay and pay hard."

"That could definitely be part of it," she admitted. "But the bodies had been staged as a taunt to me. The killer wants me involved in this investigation."

Harley looked at her again. "You think I was the target? That the gunshots were a warning for me to back off. FYI, I won't," he insisted.

There'd been no need for him to say that last part, and if the killer knew Harley, he'd be aware of that as well. "This shooting will make the news," she spelled out a moment later. "No way to keep this under wraps, and it'll come out that the sheriff of Silver Creek, his deputy and a Texas Ranger were here to investigate a serial killer."

As if on cue, her phone dinged with yet another text from her father. Ava ignored it, but she couldn't ignore the knock at the door. She groaned because she figured her father had certainly found her, but when Harley answered it, she saw it was Theo.

Theo's attention went straight to her. "I just saw the EMT and she said she'd given you a checkup. I wasn't sure if you'd be dressed or not."

"It was just a heartbeat check for the baby. Everything is fine," Ava explained, and she immediately shifted gears. "Please tell me the Austin cops have found Aaron."

"They didn't have to," Theo informed her. "Because Aaron just showed up here."

Of all the things Ava thought he might say, that hadn't been one of them. "He's turning himself in? Has he confessed?" She would have added even more questions had Theo not held up his hand to stop her.

"No confession. He claims he's the victim, that someone is trying to set him up so it looks as if he tried to kill you. He says he's here to set the record straight."

Ava had to take a couple of moments to process that. "Does Aaron know who I am?"

Theo nodded. "He mentioned you by name."

"I want to talk to him," she insisted.

"Me, too," Harley piped in.

"Figured you would, and Lieutenant O'Malley is going to give you a few minutes with him." Theo motioned for Harley and her to follow him. "Aaron's been Mirandized, so he might just clam up and wait for a lawyer. If that happens, then the lieutenant doesn't want us pressing Aaron on anything."

Ava understood because that kind of pressure could hurt with a conviction. "Is there enough to arrest Aaron?" she asked as they walked down a long corridor lined with interview rooms.

Theo stopped outside one of the doors and shook his head. "Aaron consented to a gunshot residue test, and it came back negative."

That didn't mean the man hadn't recently fired a gun, especially if he'd fired a rifle, but since he'd agreed to the test, it likely meant he knew he was going to be clean.

"Can any witnesses put Aaron on the roof of that building where the shots were fired?" Harley asked, keeping his voice low.

"Not so far, and Aaron told Lieutenant O'Malley he was in the area so he could visit Caleb. He'd parked up the street and claims he was walking to Caleb's apartment when the shots started. The Austin cops found his car and verified that it would have been the nearest parking since all the visitor spots were filled for the parking lot at Caleb's building."

Ava groaned because that was a plausible explanation. Not necessarily a truthful one but being in the vicinity of a shooting wasn't enough to arrest the man. If Aaron was the killer, she could only hope he'd say something incriminating that could be used to hold him.

"Marnie said Aaron had told her that Caleb had threatened him," Ava reminded them. "It's possible Marnie got it wrong, but if Aaron came here to try to silence Caleb, he might have planned on shooting him."

Harley made a sound of agreement but then shook his head. "Caleb came outside his apartment after the shots started, but the gunman still continued firing at us."

True. That was possibly some kind of ploy. Ava couldn't wrap her mind around it just yet, but she intended to give it plenty of thought.

"I'm going to insult you by asking you if you're sure you're up to talking with Aaron," Theo told her. "You could just watch from observation if you want."

Ava wasn't insulted. Okay, maybe she was a little. "I'm a cop. If I can't be objective, I'll just keep quiet and let Harley and you do the questioning."

Theo nodded in approval, opened the door and they went in.

Aaron wasn't seated at the lone table in the room. He was pacing, and he came to an abrupt stop, his eyes spearing hers.

"Ava," he said, looking her over, his attention stopping only briefly when he noticed her baby bump.

"Aaron," she *greeted* back.

The past twenty years hadn't been kind to the man. Even though he wasn't yet forty, there was plenty of gray in his sandy-blond hair, and his thin almost gaunt face was lined with wrinkles.

As she'd done with Caleb, she looked for any hatred or venom aimed at her, but she didn't see it. Maybe because Aaron was good at keeping it concealed. Or maybe because it wasn't there. Still, he was a suspect, and even though they'd once been in love, Ava had no intentions of letting the past sway her opinion of him.

Especially since the past might be at the root of the murders.

"You look good, Ava," Aaron commented. "And you got that badge you always wanted." He shifted his attention to Harley, who was standing side by side with her. "Is this your husband?"

"No," she replied and kept it at that.

Even though Aaron didn't add more to his question, she could see that he sensed Harley and she were together, and Aaron didn't seem ready to say anything snarky. Such as, *Are you going to keep this baby after you gave up ours?* Nope, no snark. But he shook his head the way a person did when they couldn't believe something was happening to them.

"Your daddy would pitch a fit if he found out we're here together in the same room," Aaron commented.

Edgar would indeed, but Ava didn't confirm that. "You've been in touch with my father?"

"No." His answer was firm and fast. "Last time I saw him, he said he'd have my butt thrown in jail if I didn't get out of town." He paused a heartbeat. "The last time I saw you, you were pregnant then, too," Aaron remarked. While it seemed an odd thing to say, Ava thought he might have been going for some levity because he gave a small smile.

Since there was nothing to smile about, Ava launched right into what she wanted to ask him. "Did you fire shots at me about an hour ago?"

Aaron groaned and then scrubbed his hand over his face. "Hell, no." He looked at both Theo and Harley—specifically at their badges—and repeated his denial. "Like I told the other cops, I was there to see Caleb." His attention went back to Ava. "Did you see him?"

She took her time but finally nodded.

Aaron smiled again. "Did he look like us? What did he say? I've talked to him on the phone, but I've never met him."

Ava ignored that and went with another question. "Why did you come to Austin to visit him today?"

Aaron wasn't so quick to answer this time. "Because of you. Marnie called me and said you were looking for me. I figured you wanted to talk about Caleb, so I came to Austin to introduce myself and let him know you might be in touch with him." He paused again. "All right, I just wanted him to hear my side of the story about what happened. I would have never given him up for adoption if I'd had a way of keeping him."

She considered not only his words but his tone. What she didn't hear was any of the concern Marnie had mentioned about Aaron being worried that Caleb might try to hurt him.

"And you thought I had a way of keeping him, gave him up anyway and that I might try to put some of that blame on you?" she asked.

"Maybe," Aaron conceded.

So, there was some anger for her, but Ava couldn't tell if it was enough for him to kill. "Was Caleb threatening you in any way?"

Aaron pulled back his shoulders. "Did he tell you that?" he demanded.

"Did Caleb threaten you in any way?" Harley repeated.

Aaron glared at him, but it seemed to Ava that he quickly tried to rein that in. He had to know he was under suspicion, and since he had a police record, he also knew it was best not to clash with a Texas Ranger.

"No, Caleb didn't threaten me," Aaron finally answered. "And I want to know what made you think he had."

Ava lifted her shoulder. No way would she spill what Marnie had told her, but Aaron might soon be able to figure it out since he'd already mentioned he'd spoken with Marnie. Ava also gave Theo a subtle gesture so he could proceed with the things he needed to get out of the way.

Theo took out his notepad and turned it to a fresh page, one with only the dates of the murders and not any of Caleb's notes. "Do you have solid alibis for those nights?" Theo asked.

Aaron looked over the list and his eyes registered the shock when he turned not to Theo but to Ava. "I know how this works. There were crimes committed on those dates—"

"Murders," Theo interrupted.

"'Murders'?" Aaron repeated, his gaze sweeping over all of them. "You think I killed somebody?"

"I'd like to know if you have alibis for those nights," Theo stated.

That obviously rattled Aaron. He shook his head, muttered some raw profanity under his breath and took the notepad. Because Ava was watching him, some of the color drained from his face.

"I was at Marnie's on these dates," Aaron finally said.

"You can recall where you were two and three months ago?" Ava asked, and she didn't bother to take the skepticism out of her voice. Most people had to consult a calendar to recall such things.

Aaron's eyes narrowed. "I remember because the first date was the four-month anniversary of Christina's death, and Marnie and I were both having a hard time. The second one was Christina's birthday. Last night, I was at Marnie's to pick up some pictures that Marnie thought I'd want."

"Did you stay the entire nights with Marnie?" Harley asked.

"Yeah, I would have been drinking," Aaron muttered while he looked at the dates on the notepad again. "It wasn't safe to drive so I crashed in her guest room."

That meant Aaron had been at Marnie's when Ava had been talking to the woman on the phone. Well, maybe he had, if Aaron was telling the truth.

"Let me check and see if Marnie will verify that," Theo said, stepping outside the interview room to make the call.

"I didn't kill anybody," Aaron repeated to Harley and her. "I know it looks bad because I was in Austin during this shooting, but if I'd wanted you dead, I would have gone after you a long time ago."

That put some ice in her blood and, while that seemed to be logical on the surface, there was another factor here. Christina's death. It could have triggered Aaron to want to do something to get back at the world. Or, more specifically, to get back at her for the old wrongs that had been done to him. Yes, those wrongs had been her father's doing, but maybe punishing and ultimately killing her was the way for Aaron to get back at Edgar.

"Have you told anyone about me having your baby when I was a teenager?" Ava asked.

"Christina knew," he readily admitted. He paused, his mouth suddenly a little unsteady. "She was sorry that I hadn't been able to raise my son, so she wanted to have a baby. I thought maybe that would be a good thing, and I told her if she stayed clean for six months, we'd try." He shook his head and groaned. "According to the medical examiner, Christina was about four weeks pregnant when she died."

Oh, mercy. Hearing that could have definitely been a trigger for Aaron.

"I'm sorry," Ava told him, and she meant it.

She couldn't imagine losing the baby she was carrying. Couldn't imagine having something bad happen to Caleb. But someone obviously wanted bad things for him because they'd tried to set him up by leaving that note with the bomb.

"Were you aware that my father had a PI following you?" Ava asked. Again, she studied his response to see how much alarm that would cause Aaron.

It caused him plenty.

"When?" Aaron demanded.

"Recently," she supplied. She didn't add that the PI hadn't been on Aaron during the murders, and she recalled Duran explaining that was because the investigator hadn't been able to find him. Ironic since Aaron was claiming to have been at Marnie's on three separate occasions. So, either her father's PI had simply missed spotting Aaron on those dates or someone was lying.

Aaron muttered some profanity. "I don't have to ask why your SOB of a father would do that," he snarled. "He's worried I'll rat him out. And I've thought about doing just that over the years. Trust me, I've thought of doing a lot of things—"

His tirade came to a quick stop, and Ava wished it hadn't because it had seemed as if Aaron had been on the verge of spilling something. She didn't get a chance to press him on it, either, because Theo came back into the room and immediately speared Aaron with his cop's glare.

"I just talked to Marnie," Theo stated, "and

she said she's not sure if those are the dates you stayed over at her house. In other words, she can't confirm your alibis."

Ava got a jolt of the firestorm of emotions that raced through her. If Aaron had lied about being at Marnie's, then he could have also lied about why he was here in Austin.

And it soared him to the top of their suspect list.

Aaron cursed again, but this time it wasn't muttered. It was raw and vicious. "Marnie." He spat her name out like a continuation of the profanity. "She's lying. She has to remember I was over at her place for Christina's birthday and the anniversary of her death. Hell, Marnie invited me over there for those dates."

Theo lifted his shoulder and the gesture conveyed he wasn't the least bit convinced with Aaron's denial. "Why would Marnie lie about something like that?" he asked.

"Because she hates my guts, that's why," Aaron insisted. "Marnie's always thought I should have done more to help her sister stay off drugs. I tried my damnedest to do that, but Christina just couldn't quit. Marnie never got that, and she blamed me when Christina died."

Ava worked that explanation through her mind and immediately saw a flaw in Aaron's logic. "If Marnie hates you, then why would she have allowed you to come to her house, much less stay there, as you've claimed."

Oh, if looks could kill, Aaron would have blasted her to smithereens. *"Claimed,"* he snapped. "You think I'm guilty. You think I murdered those women. Well, I didn't."

Ava was ready to pepper him with a few more questions. Ready to try to hit Aaron's hot buttons to get him to blurt out something that might end up incriminating him. She hadn't remembered Aaron having much of a temper when they'd been teenagers, but considering the life he'd led, it could have turned him bitter, and bitterness often manifested itself as rage.

"You want to know who's capable of these murders?" Aaron asked before she could continue. He didn't wait for any of them to respond. "Marnie, that's who. You're looking for a killer? Well, look straight in Marnie's direction."

Chapter Seven

Harley pulled Ava's car to a stop in front of her house and waited for her to open the garage. After she had, they went through the same security precautions they'd taken the night before. Searching her house again with weapons drawn had to be another jolting reminder of just how dangerous her life had become.

And exhausting.

Harley had seen the signs of fatigue from the spent adrenaline and the lack of sleep the night before. That's why he'd hoped she would nap on the drive back to Silver Creek, but she'd instead spent the time on her phone, trying to get updates on the Austin PD investigation. Specifically, trying to learn if the cops there could dig up enough to arrest Aaron for either the shooting or the murders.

Harley wasn't betting on either.

Simply put, there was no evidence to link Aaron to the crimes, and even with Marnie unable or unwilling to confirm his alibis, the cops would need to find some kind of smoking gun, maybe a literal one, to get any charges to stick.

During the drive, Theo had used his hands-free to try to get some updates of his own, but he wasn't having any better luck than Ava was. He'd had a fellow Ranger dig into Marnie's background, to see if she was the kind of woman who would lie about Aaron's alibis. Or if she was a woman who could really kill, but the only indication of that was Marnie's devotion to her sister.

Maybe extreme devotion.

That info had come up when Harley had questioned the Bulverde cop, Sergeant Gideon Gonzales, who'd been in charge of the investigation into Christina's death. According to Gonzales, Marnie had been beyond distraught over her sister's death. Marnie had been hysterical and sobbing in the first interviews he'd done with her, and then when he'd gone out to her house to tell her that Christina's death had been ruled an accidental overdose, Marnie had demanded that he arrest someone, that her sister's death wouldn't go unpunished.

Wouldn't go unpunished was something that definitely stuck in Harley's head, and it made him wonder if Aaron was right about the woman being capable of committing three murders. Especially if those murders got pinned on Aaron, the man Marnie might blame for losing her beloved sister.

"This part of the house is clear," Ava called out to him.

Like before, she'd taken the main living area, and since the bedrooms were clear as well, Harley made his way back to her. His main objective was to get her something to eat and then try to talk her into resting, but Ava had already poured herself a large glass of milk.

"There's sandwich stuff in the fridge," she offered.

He took her up on that, grabbing the items to make not one but two sandwiches so that Ava could eat as well. It was impossible to make himself stop worrying about her and the baby, though he doubted Ava wanted any TLC from him.

But Harley rethought that when she turned to him.

Their gazes met and he saw not only the fatigue but something else. Something he couldn't quite decipher until she spelled it out for him.

"Thank you for being here," she said. "I know we have our differences, but I really don't want to be alone in the house right now."

Yeah, he got that. Even though she was a good cop, she was still a mother-to-be, and that played into this. She could lay down her life for the badge, it was something good cops did, but she hated the risk to their child.

Harley was right there on the same page with her.

He set aside the sandwich stuff, went to her and took hold of her shoulders. He'd hoped to come up with just the right thing to say to ease some of the tension he could feel in her muscles. But her breath broke and Ava went into his arms as if she belonged there.

There'd been a time not that long ago when she would have hugged him, and more, but he could tell this particular embrace was costing her. Because this wasn't out of lust, wasn't the start of some hot foreplay that would lead them straight to bed. This was her leaning on him, and part of her would see that as a weakness.

It wasn't.

Because part of him was leaning on her, too. He needed this; the contact that gave him assurance that the baby and she were alive. Now it was up to both of them to make sure things stayed that way.

Harley didn't dare speak for fear it would cause her to move away from him. He just held her and hoped it would give her as much comfort as it was giving him.

Unfortunately, having her body pressed against his was also giving him some flashbacks of the times they'd had sex. Definitely not images he wanted in his head right now, but no matter how much he tried to fight them off, they came anyway. Still, he didn't move other than to try to give her a reassuring rub on her back.

After several long moments, Ava finally leaned away from him. Not far though. Their bodies were still touching when she looked at him.

"It's wrong for me to lean on you like this," she said, sighing. And she broke the contact for real then by stepping away.

"It's not wrong," he assured her. "You've had a really bad day. Added to that, you met your son and had to interview your ex. I think that means you've earned all the leaning you want."

The corner of her mouth lifted in the briefest of smiles, but she didn't move back toward him. Instead, she picked up her glass of milk and continued to drink. That's when he noticed her hands were trembling a little. It was barely any movement, but for Ava, it might as well have been an earthquake of a reaction.

Hell.

All of this was tearing her apart. Harley would have gone to her to try to do something about that, but her phone rang.

She groaned when she looked at the screen. "It's my father."

Great. Just what she didn't need on top of everything else. "You want me to talk to him?" Harley offered. Verbally blasting Edgar might help burn off some of this restless energy he'd gotten from the hug.

"No, but thanks," she answered. Ava took the call and put it on speaker.

"I've been in committee meetings all day, and I get out to learn that someone tried to kill my daughter," Edgar immediately snarled. "Any reason I didn't hear about it from you?"

"I've been busy," she informed him. In contrast to Edgar's fiery tone, hers was low level. Probably because she was too tired to work up a snit as her father had.

"Too busy to let me know about an attack," Edgar countered. "Too busy to give me a heads-up? I had to learn about the shooting from a reporter."

So, the press had picked up on that. Harley fired off a text to let Theo know that Silver Creek might soon be getting a share of reporters out looking for a story about the senator's cop daughter. Theo wouldn't give them that story, but at least he'd be prepared before the first one showed up.

"Yes, too busy," Ava confirmed. "I had to give my statement to the Austin PD and then I got tied up with the investigation."

She didn't add more. Nothing about Caleb or Aaron. She was no doubt waiting to see how much her father knew about all of this.

Or to maybe learn if Edgar had been involved in some way.

Edgar, however, stayed quiet for several long moments, maybe because he'd been hoping Ava would be the one to do the spilling. It must have occurred to him, though, that wasn't going to happen because the man finally huffed.

"I have contacts in Austin PD, so I know you met with Aaron Walsh," Edgar finally said. "And I know where you were when those shots were fired at you. Did Aaron try to kill you, or did he put his spawn up to doing it?"

Oh, that was so not the right thing to say, and Harley saw the anger whip through Ava's eyes. "My son's name is Caleb. If you use that disgusting term again, I'm hanging up. Now, tell me what the heck it is you want so I can end this conversation and eat."

Maybe Edgar was weighing his options because he went quiet again. "All right, I'll tell you what I want." Obviously, his brief silence hadn't toned down his own anger, because he then used the mean-as-a-snake tone that suited him so well. "I want you and your fellow cops to be more discreet when dragging me into this investigation.

I had nothing to do with those shots being fired, nothing to do with the murders."

Ava's forehead bunched up. "What do you mean dragging you into this investigation? Are you doing general griping about that, or is there something specific?"

"Something specific," he snapped. "The sheriff you work for called Valerie Chandler and my campaign manager so he could verify that I had alibis for the dates of the murder. He wanted alibis from me." Edgar's voice rose on that last bit, said in a way that he felt he was above the law for such things.

He wasn't.

And Harley decided to let him know that.

"Senator, your daughter could have been killed today," Harley spoke up. "I'd think you'd want to do anything and everything possible to make sure her attacker is caught. That means providing pesky info to law enforcement so they can do their jobs. That also means the cops interviewing your longtime social companion, Valerie Chandler, so you can be ruled out as a potential suspect in three murders."

"Harley," Edgar grumbled, stretching out his name. "Of course, you'd be with my daughter. Why the hell didn't you stop shots from being fired at her?"

Ava huffed and moved as if to end the call,

but Harley waved her off. Edgar was riled, and they might get something out of all this ranting.

"Harley put himself in between me and the shooter," Ava informed her father. "Unfortunately, Harley doesn't have wings or a superhero power, so he couldn't fly to the top of the building and dissolve the shooter with his laser vision."

"He shouldn't have put you in the position where you could have been shot in the first place," Edgar fired back. "If you hadn't insisted on seeing…that young man, you wouldn't have been such an easy target."

Well, at least Edgar had refrained from using the *spawn* word again, but Harley couldn't tell if the man's anger was because he was genuinely worried about Ava's safety or because of the bad publicity this might generate. Maybe it was some of both, but considering this was Edgar, the publicity was definitely a big factor.

"Why did you go see that young man anyway?" Edgar pressed a moment later.

"I figured your sources would have told you that," Ava countered.

"Is it because he's a suspect in the murders?" Her father threw it out there.

Ava dragged in a long breath. The weariness was coming back in her expression, and Harley so wished he hadn't stopped her from hanging up on this dirtbag father of hers.

"We questioned him," Ava said. "And he's not a suspect. That's because he fully cooperated with the police and didn't whine to me that he was being treated unfairly. Ironic, since he of all people could have claimed mistreatment at his bio-mother being forced to give him up or else see his bio-father arrested."

"That wasn't mistreatment," Edgar stormed. "It was the right thing to do. I was trying to save you, and look what you did. You ended up throwing your life away by pinning on that badge and bedding a damn Texas Ranger—"

Ava hit End Call, and Harley could see the visible effort she had to make to steady herself. She didn't get long to do that, though, because within seconds, her phone rang again.

"I'm going to block him," she muttered, but when she looked at the screen, a different kind of tension crossed her face. "It's Theo. Is everything all right?" she immediately asked. She put this call on speaker, too.

"No one else has been shot at or murdered," Theo let her know. "I'm just calling to give you a heads-up that your father might be getting in touch with you."

Ava frowned. "I just got off the phone with him."

"Ah. Well, he was fast. I'll bet he was mad because I talked to Valerie Chandler and Duran."

"Bingo," Ava verified. "Please tell me there's some inconsistencies you can use to open an investigation on one of them."

"Nothing on Edgar. His alibis checked out. Apparently, Valerie spends a lot of nights at his place, and she was there all three of the nights of the murders. Her driver dropped her off and picked her up the following mornings, and he confirmed that she was at that location."

"Is it possible Edgar left when she was asleep?" Harley asked.

"Possible but not likely. Valerie claims to be a light sleeper and insists she would have known if Edgar had left the bed. Also, once I pressed Edgar, he said he'd provide me with security footage to prove he arrived at and didn't leave the premises on the nights of the murders. Oh, and of course, he demanded I keep the footage private or he'd sue me."

Yep, that sounded like Edgar. It also sounded as if his alibis were fairly solid. Considering that Caleb's had checked out, too, both men had moved way down on their suspect list. However, there was one person directly connected to Edgar who was still firmly a suspect.

"What about Duran's alibis?" Harley asked.

"His aren't nearly as airtight as Edgar's," Theo

explained. "In fact, he doesn't have one for two of the nights. Claimed he was home alone and, unlike Edgar, he doesn't have any security footage that might substantiate that. For one of the other nights, the last one, Duran was on the phone with a colleague who will confirm he had a lengthy conversation with Duran."

"Duran could have been on the phone while he was in Silver Creek," Ava quickly pointed out.

"Yep, and that's why I've asked Duran to voluntarily give me his phone records. He said he needed to consult with his attorney first."

That sounded like a possible red flag. Possible. But there were also people who didn't automatically cooperate with law enforcement even if that cooperation would help clear their name and catch a killer.

"If I don't have Duran's phone records by tomorrow," Theo went on, "I'll press to get a warrant. That won't be easy," he added. "Because I'm sure Duran has contacts in high places."

True, but he wasn't a senator, and Edgar could possibly be persuaded to press Duran to cough up the records. *Might.* Edgar and Duran were close, but since Edgar had had his privacy violated, he might insist his campaign manager do the same. Edgar might especially go for that if it gave him some good press to prove he was cooperating with the investigation.

"I just got an update from Austin PD on the shooting," Theo advised. "There was no rifle on the building. Nor was one found in the general area. There are no witnesses who can put Aaron on that roof."

That didn't mean, though, that Aaron hadn't been there and fired those shots. "How'd the shooter get up on that building?" Ava asked.

"Probably used the fire escape. Unless he was up there all night, it means he went up in broad daylight, but the back of the building doesn't have any visibility from any of the streets that crisscross that area."

Still, that was a gutsy move. Unless the shooter blended in so well that no one would have been suspicious. With Caleb ruled out, Harley went with another possibility.

"The shooter could have been a hired gun," Harley interjected, throwing it out there. "If so, then he was hired to purposely miss us because he would have had a clean enough shot of Ava, you or me when we left Caleb's apartment."

Both Ava and Theo made a sound of agreement. "The motive could have been just to terrorize me," Ava added. "Or to make us believe it was connected to Caleb. Even though Caleb couldn't have fired the shots, the shooter might have wanted us to believe he was trying to silence us for something Caleb might have told us."

Yes, and that took them back to Aaron. "Is there anything Caleb could have said that would have incriminated Aaron in some way? Or," Harley tacked onto that, "incriminated any of our suspects?"

Ava clearly didn't know because she shook her head. "Nothing I can think of," she conceded, spelling it out. "But I might not be the best judge of that."

She didn't spell out that it was hard to be objective about her own son, but Theo picked up on it.

"How are you dealing with all of this?" Theo came out and asked.

She paused a long time. "I'm not sure. What I'm feeling for him is getting mixed up with the attack and the murders. I considered asking him to come and stay here so I can better protect him, but since I'm the target, that would be like putting him straight in a path of danger."

Harley couldn't argue with that. Apparently, neither could Theo.

"The Rangers are keeping an eye on Caleb," Harley reminded her. And, while that wasn't a foolproof plan, the alternative was sending Caleb to a safe house. That might still happen if there was even a hint of an attack aimed at him.

"And I'm keeping in regular contact with both the Rangers and Austin PD," Theo assured her.

"One more thing. I called Marnie on the drive back to Silver Creek, and I'm having her come in for an interview tomorrow."

"She agreed to come here?" Harley asked.

"I didn't give her much of a choice. I said there were some inconsistencies in what she reported to Ava and you, and that I needed her to clarify it face to face. Aaron might have just been tossing around accusations about Marnie to try to get himself out of hot water, but I still want to hear what the woman has to say. If she truly does hate Aaron, he could be right about her trying to set him up for the murders."

Harley tried to work that out in his mind. He'd read Marnie's bio and knew she'd once taught martial arts, so it was possible she would have been strong enough to abduct and kill three women. Strong enough to pose them, too. But for Marnie to set something like this in motion, it meant she's known all about Aaron and Ava having a child together. Maybe that was something Aaron had revealed during one of his self-confessed drunken talks with the woman. Or, if he'd told Christina, she could have passed along the info to her sister.

"Marnie is coming in at nine tomorrow morning, and I told her she was more than welcome to bring a lawyer with her," Theo added. "I'd like you both in the interview room."

"We'll be there," Ava assured him as Theo ended the call.

Ava's sigh was long and weary, and she continued to stare at the phone for several more seconds. "Whoever's behind the murders and the attack today...why didn't he or she just directly come after me since I'm almost certainly the intended target?"

Harley had already given this plenty of thought and he kept going back to one point. "Maybe the killer is waiting for you to have the baby. After all, none of the other three victims were pregnant."

That didn't help the weariness in her eyes. "So, four more months of murders and then me. If that's true, I guess I should be thankful that the serial killer doesn't want to harm our baby."

The "our" caused his stomach to jitter because it made them sound like a unit—which they were. For parenting anyway. Harley was hoping that was a start. Even if Ava and he were never lovers again, he wanted her to at least be in the same room with him without tensing up.

"Duran, Aaron and Marnie," she muttered, obviously leaving that "our" behind. "There's also the possibility my father could have hired someone." Ava stopped, shook her head, obviously rethinking that. "No, he wouldn't have needed to hire anyone. Not when Duran will do anything and everything for him."

"Good point. And, rather than risk anyone finding out what was happening, Duran could have done the murders himself."

Even though he'd been in law enforcement for well over a decade, it was still hard for Harley to wrap his mind around calculated murder. Especially murders like these that were meant to send a message and not because the actual victims had given the killer cause to murder them.

Ava stayed quiet a moment, but Harley could see the tightness creep back into her body. "Edgar told me that he struck a deal with you."

She couldn't have shocked Harley more if she'd slapped him. "What?" he demanded, his shoulders snapping back.

Ava took another moment and she pinned her cop's eyes to him. "My father's exact words were *I struck a deal with that bedmate Ranger of yours.* He said there'd be no charges against him and that his name would be cleared within the hour. And his name was indeed cleared."

Harley was shaking his head before she even finished. "I made no such deal, not with him or anyone else I've ever investigated. That's not how I work, and you know it."

"He had me listen to a recording of a conversation between the two of you. In it, you said he'd be cleared, that you'd make sure of it." She stopped, cursed. "He could have doctored the recording."

"Damn right he could have, or taken it out of context." Harley groaned and wanted to join Ava in that cursing. "Is that why you split with me?"

"It played a part in it," she admitted. "But so did the pregnancy itself. I figured if we were together, you'd feel obligated to do something. Like propose or suggest we move in together for the sake of the baby. I didn't want that."

He opened his mouth to say that wouldn't have happened, but Harley had to admit that, yes, it would have. He would have certainly offered marriage, and while he'd had deep feelings for Ava, she would have known the proposal had only come because she was pregnant. No way would she have accepted, so it'd just been easier for him to keep her at arm's length.

"Edgar told you that lie to put a wedge between us," Harley spelled out. He would have pressed for a heart-to-heart that he thought they should have now, but her phone rang again.

It wasn't Theo's or her dad's name on the screen this time. It was Candice Barlow, Ava's nearest neighbor.

"She probably heard about the shooting and wants to make sure I'm okay," Ava muttered, answering the call on speaker.

"Ava," the woman immediately said, and Harley had no trouble hearing the distress in her voice. "I was just looking out my kitchen window and I think—" She broke off and a hoarse sob tore from her mouth. "Oh, God. Ava, I think there's a body on your back porch."

Chapter Eight

A body.

Ava had thought this day couldn't possibly get
any worse, but she'd obviously been wrong.

"I think it might be a woman's body," Candice continued. "I didn't want to get any closer
to see for sure—"

"Stay inside your house," Ava instructed. "I'll
check it out."

"Not alone, dear. Please not alone. I can call
the sheriff," her neighbor offered.

"I'm not alone. Harley Ryland is with me." No
need for Ava to explain that Harley was a Texas
Ranger. In a small town like Silver Creek, everyone already knew that. "Just stay inside," she
repeated, ending the call.

And drawing her gun.

Harley had already drawn his, and stooping
low so his head wouldn't be an easy target from
her kitchen window, he went closer so he could
look. Then he cursed.

"Not a body," Harley assured her. "It's just a mannequin head, like the ones that people put wigs on. There's a garbage bag, but it doesn't appear to have anything in it." He paused a heartbeat. "It has a mask of your face."

That knocked some of the air out of her. So, this had been left by the killer or at least by someone who had unreported details of the case. A sick prank, and it meant the killer had been right here, right at her home.

"Don't go out there," Ava muttered.

No need for her to spell out this could be a trap to lure them outside to be gunned down. Even though she, technically, lived in town, there was a heavily wooded greenbelt area behind her house that separated the residential area from the park, which had a lot of trees and trails. The killer could be waiting out there, hiding in those trees.

"I'm calling Theo," Harley let her know, keeping his attention on the backyard while he did that.

Staying to the side, Ava went to the window and had a look for herself. At first glance, it definitely did appear to be a body, and it would have especially seemed that way from Candice's house. But Ava immediately saw the white Styrofoam neck, the only part that was visible what with the garbage bag and the mask.

The mask was identical to the other three.

Oh, yes, that knocked more of the air from her lungs. She'd considered that it would have been risky for someone to haul a body from those woods to her porch, but it wouldn't have been that hard to bring in just the head, garbage bag and mask.

"Theo's on his way," Harley relayed to her. "And he'll contact the CSIs."

Her mind hadn't gone there yet; that soon a team of CSIs would be combing the area. Maybe looking inside, too, even though she'd gotten no alerts of a break-in. Still, Theo would want to be thorough.

"I'm not going to ask if you're okay because I know you're not," Harley said. "But will you at least consider sitting down. You've gone pale."

Pale and a little sick to her stomach, but she knew sitting wasn't going to help with the symptoms. She was a cop and had a job to do even if right now that job was simply giving a visual assessment of the area while she waited for the sheriff to show up.

"When I got back from the murder scene in the wee hours of the morning, I didn't check the back porch," she admitted.

"Neither did I. And I didn't even glance out there when we got back today."

"Same," Ava confirmed. "I glanced out the

window when I was drinking some milk and taking my vitamin, but I didn't look down at the porch. That means, the head could have been put there at any time during the past twenty-four hours."

She could have slept while it was out there. A thought that sickened her even more. Even though it wasn't a human head, it still represented what this sick snake intended to do to her and any others on the hit list. He wanted to make them lifeless things.

And that sent a shot of pure raw anger through her.

Ava wanted to do something to stop this, and she nearly started calling neighbors to ask if they'd seen absolutely anything. But it would be a waste of time. If anyone in the neighborhood had seen anything suspicious, they would have already let her know. That probably meant the killer had put the head there when it'd been dark. Heck, maybe even after Ava had been called out to the crime scene for the third murder.

"I can take you to my house on the ranch," Harley offered.

It was tempting and, while the ranch was secure, it wasn't impenetrable. A shooter could still get to them. Plus, Ava wasn't sure running and hiding was the way to go here. In fact, drawing out the killer might be the fastest way to stop him from going after someone else.

"No," she answered, "I think it's best if we stay here. Notice that I said *we* because I know there's no way you'd leave me."

"You got that right." He glanced at her, frowning. "You're thinking of trying to use yourself as some kind of bait. You're not," he added, and there was plenty of insistence in his tone.

"I don't want another murder on my conscience," she muttered.

"It's not on your conscience. It's on the person who's doing these killings."

Harley moved closer to her and, even though he was still keeping watch, he also ran his hand down the length of her arm. For such a small gesture, it was plenty comforting.

Ava nearly broke then. She nearly gave into the despair of not being able to stop the monster who was killing and tormenting. She nearly allowed herself just to lean on Harley and let him give her all the comforting gestures in his arsenal. Since he'd once been her lover, she knew that arsenal was plenty full.

But she held back.

For one thing, if she broke, she wasn't sure she could piece herself back together any time soon. Not even with Harley's help. Added to that, she heard the vehicle pull into her driveway and knew that Theo had arrived. A moment later, she got a text confirming that.

I'll have a look around. You and Harley stay put but be ready to give me backup if needed.

Will do, she texted back.

Harley took Theo's instructions to the max by going to the back door. He opened it just a few inches, which gave him a better view of the yard and the woods. It also meant he was now in a position to fire if it became necessary.

Ava stayed at the window so she'd be able to cover the yard and woods from a different angle. She tried to pick through the trees and underbrush, but it was thick, and indeed possible that someone was out there watching and waiting.

There were the sounds of more vehicles arriving, and Ava soon spotted Deputy Jesse Ryland join Theo to observe the scene. Like Theo, Jesse was a good cop, and she was hoping they'd spot something they could use to crack this investigation and ID the killer.

Two more deputies arrived, Nelline Rucker and Cruz Molina, and Theo sent them to search the woods. Ava watched. Watched, too, as Jesse took some pictures of the fake head and then leaned in for a closer examination.

"There's a piece of paper sticking out from beneath the side of the trash bag," Jesse called out, and he looked through the kitchen window to meet her gaze. "It's a note, and it just says *Soon.*"

So, another taunt. Once again, Ava was glad she hadn't fallen apart, because she needed her anger right now. That would keep her going.

She heard yet another vehicle approach the house and figured it was the CSIs. But Ava rethought that when she saw Theo peer around the side of the house and curse.

"It's Duran," Theo relayed to her. "Any idea what he wants?"

"No," Ava said, going closer to the open door so Theo would be able to hear him. "He's never been to my house, and he didn't call ahead. My father probably sent him." Why Edgar would do that, Ava didn't know.

"You want me to get rid of him?" Theo asked her.

"No, I'll talk to him. Are there any signs of a shooter out there?"

"Not so far." Theo glanced at the two deputies who were looking through the wooded area before he pinned his gaze to Ava's. "Just remember that Duran is a suspect. Frisk him before you let him in the house. He probably won't like that, but I'd rather have you in the 'better safe than sorry' mode."

So would she, and that's why Ava gave Theo a

quick nod—just as there was a knock at the front door. Harley was right by her side, of course, when she answered it, and he didn't allow Duran to get out a single word before he pulled the man inside and checked him for weapons.

Duran was clearly surprised because he made a strangled sound of protest. "Really? Is this necessary?"

"It is," Harley assured him without missing a beat. He extracted a snub-nosed .38 from a concealed holster inside Duran's jacket and held it up. "You'd better have a license to carry concealed," he informed him.

"I do." There was plenty of indignation and anger in Duran's body language, but he didn't reach out to try to snatch back the gun. "What's going on? Why are those police cars here, and why would you have to disarm me when I just came here to talk to you?" He aimed those questions at Ava.

She debated how much to tell him but decided to go with full disclosure so she could observe his reaction. "Someone—a coward, no doubt— left a dummy's head on my porch. A coward because he wasn't man enough to confront me head-on."

Harley shot her a warning glance, obviously reminding her that he didn't want her to make herself bait. She was sort of doing that by trying to goad Duran, but the man didn't react with temper.

"You mean like a sick prank?" Duran asked.

"Exactly like a sick prank," she verified. "He was probably hoping it'd send me into an emotional tailspin so I'd do something foolish."

Ava wouldn't mention that the emotional tailspin likely would have happened had Harley not been there to anchor her.

Duran muttered something under his breath she didn't catch and shook his head as if disgusted. She reminded herself that his reaction could be faked. After all, Duran probably had to conceal a lot of what he was thinking when he was on the campaign trail with her father.

Duran glanced out the window as the CSI van arrived and he shook his head again. "What can I do to help?" he asked.

She was betting he'd had to offer that a lot, too, but Ava figured he wasn't going to like how she was about to take him up on that offer.

"You can help by truthfully answering some questions," she spelled out for him.

Duran didn't look especially offended. "Questions about what?"

"Everything," she supplied, and since this could take a while, and Ava didn't especially want to be standing in front of any windows, she motioned for them to have a seat in the living area. "Start with anything and everything you haven't told me about Aaron and Caleb, and then move on to any knowledge whatsoever you have about the murders or the shooting today in Austin."

Duran dragged in a long breath and she could see the calculation in his eyes. Oh, what to say and what to keep to himself.

"I'll arrest you for obstruction of justice if you withhold anything about this investigation," Harley threatened. "And, FYI, this is a broad investigation, and it includes anything that's happened to Ava or Aaron for the past twenty years. If you've been keeping secrets, spill them now."

Ava couldn't have said it better herself, and she matched Harley's hard stare with one of her own.

Duran volleyed glances at both of them before he sighed.

"I don't have any details about Ava's pregnancy that you don't already know," Duran started. "Edgar was furious when he found out she was pregnant, and he did tell Aaron he'd be arrested if he didn't leave town and never contact Ava again. By the way, even if that was criminally wrong, the statute of limitations has long passed. There's absolutely no reason for anyone else to know about it."

"I'll determine that," Ava said, and she made a keep-going motion with her hand.

Duran sighed again, but he did, indeed, keep going. "Edgar asked me to keep an eye on Aaron to make sure he stayed away, so I'm the one who hired the private investigators. One to monitor Aaron's whereabouts. Another to keep an eye on you."

Ava knew she shouldn't have been surprised about that last part, but it was a bit of a shock to hear it confirmed. "How long did you keep PIs on me?" She wanted to know.

"Until you went to the police academy. I figured you'd notice someone following you around, and I didn't want it to lead to a potentially embarrassing situation for your father."

There was a definite creep factor in having her under surveillance for all those years, but the PIs wouldn't have seen anything worth reporting back to Duran or her father. After she'd given up Caleb for adoption, she'd followed the straight and narrow. No boyfriends, no parties, no social stuff whatsoever. Ava had focused on her studies so she could become a cop. It had become an obsession, probably because she'd wanted to right wrongs. She could thank her father for that particular legacy.

"I want the names of the PIs," Ava ordered.

Duran reluctantly nodded. "The one who was on you died a few years ago. Pancreatic cancer. His name was Don Stewart. The one on Aaron is Darcel Harrison. He's good," Duran added. "He's been on Aaron all these years with calls and cursory checks to make sure he's staying away from you."

Harley fired off a text, no doubt to one of his fellow Rangers so they could do a background check on the PIs. Harrison would also have to be interviewed.

"Did the PI actually lose touch with Aaron after Christina's death?" Ava came out and asked.

"Yes," Duran readily answered. "For a while, anyway. Aaron lost his job and moved from his apartment, but he resurfaced a couple of months later."

"Resurfaced at Marnie's?" Ava pressed, hoping that the PI had been on Aaron when he'd visited the woman.

"No. You're wanting to know if I had Marnie's house under surveillance during the dates of the murders? I didn't," Duran supplied before Ava could confirm that was absolutely what she wanted. "I have no idea of either Marnie's or Aaron's whereabouts for those dates."

Duran stopped, but Ava could tell there was something else he was holding back. "Spill it," she ordered.

The man looked at Harley. "I'm about to tell you both something…sensitive. Something that we must keep among just the three of us."

"No," Harley said without hesitation. "If what you're withholding can catch a killer, it won't be kept hush-hush." He leaned in closer, violating the man's personal space. "Now, talk."

Duran swallowed hard and paused a long time. "Aaron has been trying to blackmail Edgar for months now. Edgar doesn't know," he quickly added. "I took the initial call from Aaron, and I'm the one who's been dealing with him."

Ava was certain the look she gave Duran was loaded with skepticism. "Someone was trying to blackmail my father, and you didn't let him know? Why would you keep something like that from him?"

"Because I didn't want Edgar to be involved in something that could be potentially construed as unsavory, possibly even criminal. Aaron demanded hush money, and I reasoned with him that he didn't have a shred of proof that Edgar had had any part in what happened twenty years ago. Aaron said he'd go to the press, and that they'd believe him. I assured him that they wouldn't, that it'd be his word against a sitting state senator."

She could see it possibly happening that way. Possibly. But she was almost positive Edgar knew. Then again, if he had, and Aaron had continued to push the idea of spilling the truth,

Aaron might have had some kind of fatal "accident" to get him completely out of the picture.

"You said Aaron had been trying to blackmail Edgar for months," Harley restated. "How long exactly? And how much have you paid him?"

Duran's mouth tightened. "Seven months." He paused again. "I gave Aaron a one-time payment of ten thousand dollars. I emphasized that was all he was going to get."

Ava zoomed right in on the seven months. "Did Aaron make the contact before or after his girlfriend's death?"

"Right before. In fact, I had the PI deliver the money in cash, and that night his girlfriend died."

Oh, mercy. That was either a horrible coincidence or else Aaron had given Christina the money to get the drugs that had killed her.

"And Aaron hasn't contacted you since about getting another round of cash?" Harley asked.

"He did," Duran admitted. "But I informed him if he pressed the matter, that I'd tell everyone he was responsible for his girlfriend's death. I believe he's worried how Marnie would react to that."

"Should Aaron be worried about Marnie?" Ava asked.

Duran's mouth tightened again. "Yes, I think he should. I've had a background check done on the woman, and Marnie practically raised her after their folks died. She was fiercely protective of Christina. She already despises Aaron, so news like this wouldn't sit well with her."

"'Protective,'" Ava repeated in a mutter. "Protective enough that Marnie would kill and try to set up Aaron?"

Duran paused again. "Possibly. But I think a stronger scenario here would be that Aaron is committing the murders with the plan to try to set up Edgar." His eyes met hers. "And Aaron could want to punish Edgar by killing you. That's why I'm begging you to take precautions, Ava. Despite your differences with your father, he loves you and doesn't want you hurt."

Ava could have debated whether or not her father was even capable of love, but Aaron might believe he was. If so, that was a fairly strong motive for murder, and Aaron might be savoring the notion of Edgar sitting on death row to pay for crimes he hadn't committed.

"May I get back my gun before I leave?" Duran asked, standing.

Harley thought about it a long time while he kept his steely stare aimed at him. He finally nodded, but he didn't hand Duran the gun until the man was out the door and on the porch.

"Duran is staying on our suspect list," Harley insisted the moment he shut the door and locked it.

He'd taken the words right out of her mouth. "I agree, because Duran could be killing with the plan to set up Aaron. If I'm dead, too, then there's no one to verify Aaron's claims of what my father did twenty years ago."

It sickened her to think that the man who'd just sat and chatted with her would want her dead, but keeping his boss out of trouble was Duran's specialty. In this case, Duran might have seen this as a perfect solution to tying up a lot of potential problems.

Her phone rang and her stomach jumped when she saw Caleb's name on the screen. She prayed he wasn't calling to tell her he'd been attacked, and she nearly fumbled her phone because she tried to answer it so fast.

"Are you okay?" she blurted out, putting the call on speaker so Harley could hear.

"I was going to ask you the same thing," Caleb answered. "Someone emailed me a picture. It looks like a mannequin's head, but it's got your face on it. I'm guessing it's some kind of mask, but it's definitely a picture of you on the mask."

Oh, mercy. Ava had hoped that Caleb wouldn't be pulled into the sick details of this. "When did you get the picture?" she asked, forcing herself to be the cop and not the mom.

"About ten minutes ago. Should I report it to the Austin police?"

"No, I'll take care of that." Or rather, Harley would, she realized, when he stepped aside to get that started. "Austin PD will send someone out to look at the email," she informed Caleb.

Though Ava was betting the killer probably wouldn't have used a server that could be traced back to him or her, they might get lucky.

"I'm sorry this happened to you," she said. "I'm sorry...for a lot of things," Ava settled for saying.

"I'm sorry for you, too." Caleb muttered some profanity. "Are you safe where you are? I mean, this killer can't get to you, can he?"

His concern touched her and she started to lose the battle she'd been having with her nerves. Her eyes watered, the tears threatening to spill.

"I'm taking precautions," she told him, giving him the best assurance she could. "You're doing the same?"

"I am. I'm taking my classes online for a few days, just until this is over. Stay safe," he added before he muttered a goodbye and ended the call.

Harley finished up his call, too, and made his way back to her. He must have seen she was on shaky ground because he immediately pulled her into his arms.

"Lieutenant O'Malley is sending an officer to Caleb's place right now," he murmured directly against her ear.

She felt the warmth from his breath, the gentle way he was holding her, and she welcomed every bit of it. And wanted more. For just a few seconds, she wanted not to be able to feel all these horrible emotions. Emotions that a killer had her son in his sights.

Ava turned and kissed him.

This was wrong. She knew it was. But didn't care. Apparently, neither did Harley because a deep sound rumbled in his throat. A sound of instant need and heat, and he returned the kiss. Not with a fiery, urgent need, but with a gentleness.

He tasted good, just as she remembered, and that savor sent an instant ache for him through her body. She automatically slid her arms around him, drawing him closer. And closer. Until they were body to body and mouth to mouth. Until Harley deepened the kiss and shot the heat and need straight through the roof.

It was that intense, clawing need that caused her to pull back. Her breath was gusting when she tore her mouth from his, and the shocking realization of what she'd just done made her want to be filled with regret.

But she wasn't.

No regret. Only the need. And that's why she'd had to pull away from him.

"I can't fall for you again," she said. "I just can't."

Because it could lead to more than just a broken heart. This time it could be the fatal distraction that got her and her baby killed.

Chapter Nine

Harley worked on the ever-growing paperwork at Ava's kitchen table while he waited for her to make a morning appearance. He could hear her in the shower, so he knew it wouldn't be long before she joined him, hopefully for breakfast and then they could leave to go to the sheriff's office for Marnie's interview.

For now, Harley welcomed the quiet moments so he could try to give himself a serious attitude adjustment. Hard to do, though, with Ava's words constantly repeating in his head.

I can't fall for you again.

That hadn't exactly been what he'd hoped to hear after the scalding kiss they'd shared. Not with the need for her skyrocketing. But he totally got where she was coming from. This was the absolute worst time for either of them to be distracted with things such as heat, need and kissing. It was there though.

Mercy, was it.

Harley knew he would have to stomp all of that down and focus on catching a killer. That was the only way to ensure Ava and their daughter were safe. Once they had this SOB behind bars and dealt with the aftermath, then maybe he could start trying to convince Ava to give that *falling for him again* a chance.

For now, he just had to work and make sure he was doing everything possible to keep her safe. Thankfully, plenty of people were doing that as well. Theo and some of the other deputies were working round-the-clock, and the CSIs had searched through every inch of Ava's yard and the woods. The plan was for the CSI team to return today to undertake a check inside her house while Ava and he were at the sheriff's office. Harley didn't expect them to find anything useful, but it was one of those things that needed to be done.

Harley had higher hopes in the usefulness department with the reports that had come in from the PI, Darcel Harrison. There were twenty years' worth, so it would take a while to go through them all. But on Duran's okay, Darcel had sent the complete file to the Rangers and copied Theo. Theo didn't have the manpower to assign someone to pore through them, but there were techs in the Ranger crime lab making the reports a high priority. After all, it could lead to catching a serial killer.

An email that popped into his in-box got his attention off Ava and back on the investigation. It was a report from Austin PD to let him know the photo sent to Caleb had been examined and that there was no traceable info on it. That's what Harley had expected, but it was still a disappointment.

That photo taunt had been plenty gutsy, and sometimes killers made mistakes when they took risks like that. Apparently, though, this killer had been smart enough to use a temporary email account and had then bounced it around servers to make it impossible to track.

Since Ava and Theo had been copied on the report, Harley figured that's what Ava was reading when she finally made her way into the kitchen. She looked up from her phone at him, their eyes locking for a couple of seconds. She didn't come out and say anything about the kiss, about why it shouldn't have happened, but he knew her well enough to know that was what she was thinking.

"You saw that the emailed photo can't be traced," she said, tipping her head to his laptop.

He nodded. "It's a dead end, but I spoke to Lieutenant O'Malley a little while ago, and we might get something new on the surveillance footage from the shooting. He's having the feed collected from any and all cameras for the surrounding block. It'll take some time, but he thinks we might be able to see someone coming or going from the scene."

Ava didn't look especially hopeful that anything would come from that, and she was probably right. Still, something eventually had to hit. It just had to. Because Harley refused to believe there was absolutely no evidence out there that wouldn't help them ID this killer.

"Did you read the report from the crime lab on the mannequin head?" he asked, already knowing the answer.

The report had come in an hour ago, and since Ava was checking for such things as often as he was, she would have already seen it. Heck, she'd likely studied it, combing for any details. But even with the combing, there just wasn't anything in it they could use. Not from this initial info anyway.

"Yes," she verified. "There's no way to trace the garbage bag, but locating the source of the mannequin head is possible."

That was it in a nutshell. What she didn't add was that finding the source for the mannequin head was a long shot, especially since the killer could have bought it online or paid cash for it at a store.

Ava looked at him again as if she might say

something of a personal nature, but her phone rang and the moment was lost. Her attention snapped to the screen and he could tell from her soft groan that this wasn't a call she wanted to take.

"It's my father," she explained. On a heavy sigh, she answered and put it on speaker. "I'm busy," she greeted, her voice snapping. That wasn't exactly a lie. They did have to leave soon for the sheriff's office for the interview with Marnie.

"So am I," her father snapped right back. "And that's why I'll make this quick. I understand Duran paid you a visit yesterday. What did he want?"

Her eyebrow lifted when her gaze met Harley's and, setting her phone down on the counter, she went to pour herself a glass of milk. "Are you saying your trusted friend and campaign manager didn't tell you why he was here?"

"He said he was checking on you," Edgar quickly fired back. "He claims you had questions about the PI I had on that scumbag who got you pregnant when you were a kid. Is that true?"

Harley didn't miss the word *claims*. So, maybe Edgar wasn't feeling a whole lot of trustworthiness for Duran.

"I'm sure Duran can tell you all about what Harley and I discussed with him," Ava replied.

"Harley," Edgar grumbled, using the same tone as he had with the scumbag referral to Aaron. "Of course, he listened in on the discussion."

"Of course," Harley interjected to let Edgar know he was listening now as well. Yeah, it was a petty dig, but Harley didn't mind resorting to pettiness where Edgar was concerned. "You tried to put a wedge between Ava and me by lying to her, by telling her I'd cut you a deal in the investigation I was running on you."

There was silence. For a long time. "You didn't charge me with anything," Edgar finally said, obviously going for some pettiness of his own. He wasn't going to own up to the lie.

And that's why Harley pushed harder.

"How do you think Ava reacted when she found out you'd lied to her?" Harley threw it out there. "How do you think my boss will react when I announce that you smeared my name for your own gain? And that gain was to make sure your daughter and I didn't end up together."

More silence, followed by a whole string of cursing. "I didn't call my daughter to be threatened by you—"

"It's not a threat. It's a guarantee," Harley assured him. "Either tell Ava the truth right now, that there was no deal cut, or I'll file a formal complaint for your allegations about me."

Even though Harley couldn't see the man's

face, he knew Edgar was seething. Ava was actually smiling while she drank her milk. Apparently, she was enjoying the pettiness, too, but underneath the enjoyment and smiles, Harley knew that Edgar's lie had done a lot of damage. It was likely the reason Ava and he weren't together right now.

"Ava misunderstood me," Edgar insisted several moments later. "I said I'd gotten a good deal what with the charges being dropped. I didn't mean for her to infer that you'd pulled strings or covered up anything. What you did was the only thing you could have done by dropping those charges because I was innocent. And now back to the reason for this call," he quickly tacked on. "Is Duran keeping something from me?"

Ava sighed. Her smile had vanished, and now there was plenty of anger in her eyes. "Ask him for yourself," she snarled for a split second before she ended the call.

She stood there a moment, probably waiting for Edgar to call back so she could decline it, but when that didn't happen, Ava's expression changed. Some of the anger vanished and in its place came the kind of look a cop got when they were trying to figure out if a suspect was telling the truth.

"Well, at least he admitted that he'd lied to me about there being a deal," she muttered. "But I think he called because this was a way of covering his butt."

"I agree." Harley couldn't say it fast enough. Edgar was a schemer, and this chat and concern about Duran could have all been a ploy. "This way, if anything leaks about Aaron, Edgar could be planning to come back with the response that he was out of the loop on that, that it was all Duran's doing." He paused and did some more thinking. "Would Duran just go along with this by taking the fall for his boss?"

"Yes," she said without hesitation. "Of course, Edgar would do everything within his power to stop Duran from being charged with anything criminal, but he would absolutely let Duran take the blame for anything that could end up reflecting badly on him."

That's the way Harley saw it, too, and it meant if it came to light about Aaron being threatened and run out of town, then Duran would likely say it'd been his doing and Edgar had had no knowledge of it.

"Did Edgar ever directly threaten Aaron back when he found out you were pregnant?" Harley asked.

She thought about that and finally shook her head. "I assumed he had, but maybe Duran is the one who delivered the message from Edgar. Of course, my father told me he'd have Aaron arrested if I didn't give up the baby. I'm sure he'd deny that, though, and he'd claim it was another misunderstanding."

True, but it would still cause some bad PR problems for the senator if all of this came out. And it would. Harley couldn't see another way around it.

"Now that Austin PD is involved with the investigation, someone will likely spill about Caleb's connection to you," Harley said. "Are you prepared for the fallout?" Because there was no way to keep it out of the media.

Again, she didn't jump to answer, and she looked directly at him before she spoke. "What if I get Caleb's permission to go ahead and leak it?" she suggested. "How do you think the killer would react to that?"

Harley blew out a long breath after he played around with some possibilities. "If the killer is Aaron, it'd likely piss him off since his plan would probably be to set up Edgar or even Duran for the murders, and he hasn't fully set that in motion."

Ava made a sound of agreement. "And, if Duran is the killer, he also hasn't had the time to set up Aaron, if that's what he has in mind." She paused. "If the killer is Marnie, then leaking this might suit her just fine because this would make Aaron the most obvious suspect."

"True," he admitted, trying to figure out the best way to word what he had to say next. "Whoever's doing these murders could be a sociopath or have some other extreme instability. You know both Aaron and Duran. Has either of them ever showed any signs that would make you believe instability could be playing into these murders?"

"I've considered it," she admitted. "Duran, yes. He has such an extreme devotion to my father that he could have crossed some very big, very dangerous lines. *Could have*," Ava emphasized. "As for Aaron, I really can't say. He had that bad-boy thing in high school, a recklessness. In hindsight, I think I was attracted to him because he was the opposite of the boys my father was pressuring me to date."

So, a rebellion of sorts. Harley wasn't jealous of Aaron. Well, probably not anyway. Ava and he weren't kids, and each of them had a past. He just didn't like the idea of thinking of Ava with another man.

So, yeah, jealousy.

"What about Marnie?" she asked. "We've only had that short conversation on the phone with her, but have you read anything in her background to indicate she could be unstable enough kill in order to get revenge?"

"Nothing so far, but if she was as devoted to her sister as Duran and Aaron have said, then

Christina's death could have tipped her over the edge." Still, there might be something he hadn't uncovered yet.

At the mention of the woman's name, Harley checked the time. "We should be getting to the sheriff's office. Theo had a cruiser dropped off right before you got in the shower, and I had it parked in your garage."

That would minimize the time Ava was outside, and therefore be a harder target for a sniper. The cruiser didn't guarantee Ava's safety, but it was one of those precautions he intended to take. Another was making sure he was near her at all times. If the killer could get to her back porch, then whoever it was could smash a window and come after her in the house.

Ava took a breakfast bar and a thermos of milk with her as they made their way to the cruiser.

Harley kept watch all around them as he pulled out of her driveway. It was broad daylight, which helped with the visibility, but since the last attack had also happened during the day, that didn't give them any level of comfort.

As Theo and he had worked out, Harley made the short drive to the sheriff's office and parked in the covered lot directly outside the door to Theo's office. It was mere steps away, but each one of them seemed to take an eternity. Harley definitely breathed a little easier once he had Ava inside.

The breathing easier hadn't lasted though.

That was because he immediately spotted one of their suspects. Harley had seen Marnie's DMV photo, so he instantly recognized her face. She was tall and had an athletic build. Some people dressed up for an interview with the cops, but not Marnie. She was wearing capris workout pants, running shoes and a loose top. She had her hair pulled back in a tight ponytail.

"What inconsistencies?" the woman demanded the moment she saw Ava and him.

Since she didn't ask who they were, Marnie must have seen photos of them, too. It wouldn't have been hard for her to find because of Ava's background and some of Harley's high-profile cases.

It took Harley a moment to recall that Theo had insisted Marnie come in for a face-to-face interview because there'd been some *inconsistencies* in what she'd said to Ava and him. And there had been. Aaron had accused Marnie of trying to set him up for the murders.

"This way," Theo said, coming out of his office and motioning for all of them to follow him.

He didn't address Marnie's question while they made their way to an interview room.

Once inside, Theo Mirandized her, causing

Marnie to gasp. "Are you arresting me?" she snapped, aiming the question at Theo.

"No. This interview is to put your statement on record. I read you your rights for your own protection, so I could remind you again that you can have a lawyer present."

"So you said when you called," Marnie muttered. Her chin came up and she looked Theo straight in the eyes when she dropped down into one of the chairs. "Well, I have nothing to hide, so ask whatever you want."

Theo, Ava and he sat as well, and Theo slid a piece of paper toward Marnie. "Look at those dates and tell me if Aaron Walsh was with you on those nights."

Marnie picked up the paper, looked at it. "I've already said I'm not sure if he was there or not. Maybe."

"Aaron claims you invited him over on those dates," Ava explained.

"I could have, in a general sort of way. You know, like drop over whenever and pick up that photo you always liked of Christina." She stopped and huffed. "Look, this isn't a big deal. I despise Aaron, but if I could say with absolute certainty that he was at my house, I would because that would give him an alibi. That's what you want, right? To make sure he has an alibi."

"Do you have alibis for those nights?" Theo asked, turning the tables on her.

Marnie gave him one sharp glare before she shook her head. "If Aaron was there, then he's my alibi, but since I can't confirm it, then I guess I don't have any. Why would I need them? I can't possibly be a suspect in the murders."

None of them confirmed that. Because she was.

"You also told us that Aaron was worried about Caleb trying to harm him," Harley threw out there a moment later. "Aaron says that's not true."

"Well, duh." Marnie dismissed that with the wave of her hand. "He said it when he was drunk and rambling. He doesn't remember a lot of things." She paused, her jaw tightening. "Like the name of the person who sold my sister the drugs that killed her."

"You think Aaron knows that?" Ava asked.

"Damn straight, I do." Marnie leaned in, her face tight with anger now. "And I also believe Aaron paid for those drugs. Instead of using the money to get her counseling help, he fed her addiction."

That meshed with what Duran had told them about the timing of the payoff he'd given Aaron. Still, Harley had searched for any connections that Aaron might have known drug dealers and he hadn't come up with anything solid.

Harley went with a different angle. He took the paper and wrote down the names of the three murdered women. "Do you know any of them?" he asked.

Marnie looked at the list and glanced up at him. Their gazes met for just a second before she looked away. "I knew the second one, Theresa Darnell. I read about her murder."

Interesting. As far as Harley knew, this was the first time one of the suspects admitted to knowing one of the victims.

"How'd you know her?" Harley pressed.

Marnie groaned and her mouth stayed tight a moment. "Aaron." She practically spat his name out. "My sister and Aaron had a lot of splits in their stormy relationship, and during one of those splits, he started seeing Theresa. I don't know how they met, so you'd have to ask him about that. Anyway, when Aaron and Christina got back together, Theresa showed up at my place looking for Aaron, and she made a big scene. I had to threaten to have her arrested before she'd leave."

Ava shook her head. "There's no police report about this."

"No, because I didn't file one. Theresa and I had words, that's all. She was looking to confront

Christina for stealing her man. A man Theresa had had for a week or two, I might point out." She added an eye roll to that.

Since Aaron almost certainly knew that Theresa's name had been one of the murdered women, Harley had to wonder why the man hadn't just volunteered that info. Because he hadn't, it made Aaron look downright guilty.

"Since you seem to be digging for anything that could put me in a bad light," Marnie went on, "you'll probably find out that one of my old boyfriends, Paul Harmon, was in a militia. One of those groups that plays soldier and stockpiles guns. When I started seeing him, I didn't know about this, and as soon as I learned of it, I broke it off."

Harley jumped right on that. "What militia and when was this?"

Marnie sighed in a way that let him know she'd been hoping they would just drop the subject with the info she'd already provided to them. "About two years ago, and I'm not sure if the group had a name or not. If they did, Paul never mentioned it to me. The only reason I'm telling you about him is because I don't want you to use that relationship to claim I have criminal ties to someone who could murder women or shoot at cops."

Maybe, but another reason could be that Marnie figured her association with this militia member would come up in a deep background check and she was hoping to make it seem unimportant. Unfortunately, some militia groups had members with expertise in explosives, so her connection was more important than she realized.

Harley looked at Theo and tipped his head to the door, silently asking if he should step out and go ahead to try to find out more about Paul Harmon. Theo gave him a nod.

"Excuse me a second," Harley said, and he went next door into the observation room so he could use the laptop there.

Harley could see and hear Theo and Ava continue the interview with Marnie, and Ava was pressing the woman to find out if she'd ever had any contact with the other two victims.

He continued to listen, but Harley started the search for Paul Harmon. There were several men with that name living in central Texas, but it didn't take Harley long to zoom in on the one who was a known member of the Brotherhood militia, a paramilitary group who dabbled in all sorts of illegal things, including gun running.

Harley couldn't immediately see that Paul Harmon had had any kind of explosives training, but that wasn't usually something that popped up in a background search, unless the guy had been arrested for explosive-related crimes. He hadn't been, which meant he needed to do some more digging. Not just into Paul but also the militia itself to make sure one of their members hadn't assisted the killer with making that bomb.

Figuring he'd gotten all he could from the cursory background check, Harley stood to go back into the interview room, but before he could leave, his phone dinged with a text from Lieutenant O'Malley at Austin PD.

The techs went through all the collected feed from the security cameras, and you need to see this particular still frame. This camera was one block from the building where the shots originated and was recorded six-and-a-half minutes from the time the last shot was fired.

Harley tapped on the image to enlarge it, figuring it would be a clearer image of Aaron. It wasn't. But Harley had no trouble whatsoever recognizing the person who'd been captured in the photo.

Hell.

It was Duran.

Chapter Ten

Duran.

Ava's mind was whirling with everything Harley, Theo and she had learned this morning. Marnie's admission that she knew one of the victims. That Aaron had as well. And that Marnie had a connection to someone who could have made that explosive device. But the bit of info that was flashing in her head like a neon sign was that Duran had been within a block of the shooting.

While Harley and she sat in the interview room they'd converted to a makeshift office, eating the lunch that'd been sent over from the diner, she again studied the image that Austin PD had managed to get for them. It was Duran all right. Not wearing his usual suit, either, but rather dressed in dark jeans and a T-shirt.

In the shot, Duran was looking over his shoulder, in the direction from where the shots had been fired. It was hard to tell from the grainy photo, but the man's face was tense, and he wasn't walking but rather running. That speed was the reason he had quickly moved out of surveillance range and another camera hadn't been able to pick him up.

What Duran hadn't had with him was a rifle, but it was possible he'd used his handgun. That would have explained the missed shots since the roof of the building had been at least fifty yards away. An expert marksman could have possibly made the shots, but Ava couldn't find any proof that Duran would qualify as an expert.

Still, the image had been enough for Austin PD to get a warrant to have the gun taken into custody and checked to see if it'd been recently fired. If it had been, and if Duran didn't have a credible reason for being in that specific area at that time, then he could be arrested.

"And what fun would that be for Austin PD," Ava muttered, causing Harley to glance up from his laptop and look at her. Like her, he was using the lunch break to continue to dig into the various threads of the investigation.

"You're talking about Duran?" he asked, obviously noticing that she was still studying the photo from the security cam.

"Yes," she confirmed. "Lieutenant O'Malley will have probably already sent someone to Duran's to retrieve the gun and question him. I suspect, first chance he gets, he'll be calling me to vent about being harassed."

"Then he can claim more harassment when Theo questions him," Harley concluded.

Duran would, certainly, but that wouldn't stop Theo from questioning the man once Austin PD was done with him. If Duran was tied to the shooting, that was Austin's jurisdiction, but anything to do with the murders would need to go through Theo.

"You should try to eat before your father shows," Harley reminded her.

True, because while Duran was in Austin being questioned, her father and Aaron would be coming to Silver Creek. Not at the same time. Sometimes, a heated verbal altercation could lead to a person saying incriminating things, but in her father and Aaron's case, the encounter could get very ugly and cause both men to lawyer up. For this phase of questioning, Theo wanted cooperation to be able to get the info to help them with those threads.

Ava took a bite of her chef's salad and checked the time. Her father was due to arrive in a half hour, but if he was angry enough, he might already be on his way. Aaron wasn't scheduled for another two hours, which would end up making this a tiring day. Then again, it'd already been tiring what with Marnie's interview and learning about Duran being spotted on the security cam.

"I got something," Harley announced, moving his burger aside so he could turn his laptop in her direction.

She immediately saw Paul Harmon's name along with the known members of the militia. Not a huge group, but there were at least a dozen of them.

"I did a cross-match of employers," Harley explained as he tapped one of the names about halfway down the list. "And Aaron worked with this guy, Lionel Henderson, at Tip Top Repairs. Aaron quit working there right before Christina's death. Around the time Duran gave him that big chunk of money. But Lionel is still employed there."

"Does he have a record?" Ava wanted to know.

"A juvie one for stealing a car. He apparently straightened up and joined the army."

She latched right onto that. "Please tell me he had explosives or demolition training."

"Bingo. He was an explosives ordnance disposal specialist. He spent six years in uniform and, from what I can tell, he got out and came back home because his mom had cancer. She died, and he joined the militia about a month later."

So, maybe his grief had driven him to be with

the wrong people. Or it could be the members of the militia were former friends.

"There are no social media posts with Lionel Henderson and Aaron, but when Aaron comes in, I'll be asking him about his former coworker."

It was definitely a connection that needed to be explored. In fact, "connections" was the theme of the new threads in this investigation.

"I wonder if Lionel Henderson ever crossed paths with any of the murdered women," Ava mused aloud. "I mean what if the murders aren't just focused on me? What if these three women got on the killer's radar because of some interaction or altercation they'd had with someone helping the killer? Someone like Paul Harmon or Lionel Henderson?"

Harley stayed quiet a moment, obviously giving that some thought. "The accomplice got to tie up some loose ends either for himself or for his boss, the killer?"

Ava nodded. "It could be a long shot, but it might apply. *Might*," she emphasized. "Because if Marnie had a run-in with Theresa, then Aaron likely could have, too. Maybe even Duran, since this would have been the time that he had a PI on Aaron. Something could have possibly happened between Duran and her to make Theresa stand out as a potential victim."

She stopped, sighed and then groaned in

frustration, waving off what she'd just said. "Or maybe the killer hadn't even put that much thought into it," Ava amended. "Maybe the only criteria he or she had was the victims were substitutes for me."

Harley stood, sighing as well, and he went to her. She was seated, but he put his hands on the arms of her chair and leaned in, looking her straight in the eyes. "We're going to catch the person responsible. We're going to stop them."

Ava so wanted to believe that. She wanted to hang on to every reassuring word Harley was doling out. Actually, she wanted to hang on to Harley himself. There must have been something in her eyes to convey that because the corner of his mouth lifted into the slightest and briefest of smiles. Then he must have remembered that part about this heat being a really bad distraction because the smile vanished.

Harley didn't move though.

He stood there, looming over her and sending off scorching vibes that heated up every inch of her. She might have leaned in and kissed him had there not been a quick knock before the door opened. Harley moved away from her as if they'd just been caught doing something wrong—which, in a way, they had.

Former sheriff Grayson Ryland was in the doorway, and even though he was now retired, he obviously still had his cop's instincts because he swept glances over both of them and asked, "Am I interrupting something?"

Ava immediately shook her head and stood. "Harley and I were just…" She stopped trying to fill in the blank with something that would only be a half-truth or an outright lie. This was Grayson, her mentor, and the man who'd been her boss for years before Theo had taken over. Grayson would see right through a lie.

"I'm frustrated and angry," Ava amended. "This snake is killing because of me, and every new piece of info only seems to complicate the investigation, not solve anything."

Grayson nodded and kept his usual unflappable expression. "You know those pieces are eventually going to come together, and you'll just keep working it until they do."

She had to cling to the hope that the "coming together" would happen, and hearing the words from Grayson made it seem like a sure thing. Theo was a darn good boss, and she had total respect for him, but Grayson was and always would be a cornerstone of the Silver Creek sheriff's office, and the new generation of Rylands were following in his footsteps. Theo was his adopted son and Harley was his adopted kid brother.

Grayson shifted his attention to Harley. "Dad and your mom wanted me to check on you." Now

Grayson smiled a little when Harley sighed and blew out a long, weary breath. "It doesn't matter how old you are, they'll still worry. You'll understand that better when your daughter is born."

Harley nodded in a way that made her think he already understood it. "I'll call them later and let them know I'm all right."

Grayson nodded as well, and looked at Ava. "Dad also wanted me to extend an invitation for you to stay at the ranch. He heard about what was left on your back porch, and he's worried about you."

Ava hadn't been able to dismiss that taunt, prank or whatever the heck it'd been, but she wasn't ready to surrender yet by leaving her home. She only hoped that wouldn't turn out to be a decision she regretted, especially since part of the reason she wanted to stay put was so the killer would eventually show himself. Or herself. That wouldn't happen if she was tucked away on the Silver Creek Ranch.

"Please tell your dad thank-you," she settled for saying. "I'll consider it."

She didn't add more because her phone rang. "It's Duran," she said when she saw the name on the screen.

Grayson muttered a quick goodbye and good luck, and he stepped back so he could close the door. Ava took the call on speaker.

"The cops just showed up at my door and are demanding my guns," Duran immediately said. "Did you put them up to this?"

"No, but it's a great idea since we now know you were in the vicinity of the shooting in Austin and could have been the one to fire those shots at Harley and me. Did you try to kill us?" Ava came out and asked.

"Of course not," Duran insisted, but Ava had no idea whether or not he was telling the truth. If he was lying, maybe the Austin cops would be able to trip him up and ultimately get a confession.

"Then why were you there during the shooting?" Harley pressed. He didn't add more, maybe waiting to see if Duran was going to deny it.

He didn't.

Duran groaned. "I was in Austin because I was following Aaron. I got a heads-up from the PI, Darcel Harrison, that Aaron intended to make a trip to Austin to see Caleb. I knew you were heading there to interview the young man, and I wanted to be on hand in case things turned ugly."

The whole explanation sounded rehearsed, which it no doubt had been. She didn't press him on how the PI had found out about Aaron going to Austin, but she wouldn't put it past Duran to have managed to plant eavesdropping devices in Aaron's residence.

"Look, I'm giving the cops my guns so they can test them or whatever," Duran went on, "and you'll soon have proof that none of them has been recently fired. I didn't shoot at Harley and you. I didn't try to kill you."

Ava heard the confidence in the man's voice about the firearms and silently groaned. Because, of course, if Duran was the shooter, he would have already gotten rid of the weapon. And that meant there was little chance of them finding it.

"I didn't actually reach the apartment building where Harley and you were," Duran added a moment later. "I was walking there from the car park, and when I heard the shots, I stayed put for a while. Then I turned and ran back to my car after I heard the police sirens. I figured I wouldn't be able to help if I arrived on scene."

He'd no doubt rehearsed that part, too. All very pat. And, worse, it might all be very true. Ava had wanted to hear something, anything, that would clue her in that Duran had been there to kill her, but she hadn't.

Not yet anyway.

"Tell me about Theresa Darnell." Ava threw the name out there.

Duran didn't jump in with a quick answer, but she thought she heard him mutter something under his breath. Profanity maybe. "I'm guessing you found out she was once involved with Aaron."

"Yes, and I'm wondering why you didn't mention it to me sooner," Ava snapped. "The woman was murdered, and you didn't think I'd want to know that she'd had a connection to Aaron. And to you," she tacked on.

"Wait a minute," he protested. "I didn't have a connection with her. I simply read about her in a report that the PI sent me."

Ava went with a theory that was starting to form. "If you thought that Aaron had spilled anything to Theresa about Caleb or what Edgar and you did, you might have been worried that she'd be angry enough to tell someone. Someone who'd be willing to make sure it hit the media."

"That didn't happen." Duran sounded adamant about that. Again, though, Ava wasn't sure if this was part of the façade that he was so very good at creating. "Yes, I had the PI keep an eye on her for a while. And, no, he didn't see who killed her. He just listened in case she started making waves to get back at Aaron. She didn't, so end of story."

Maybe, but Ava would keep digging, and there might be something in the PI's report about it.

"How about Monica Howell and Sandy Russo?" she continued, giving him the names of the other two murdered women. "Do you have a connection of any kind to either of them?"

His silence let her know that she'd hit pay dirt. "I don't have a personal connection, no. But Sandy Russo and Theresa, they knew each other. Apparently, they went to the same school, and the PI reported they'd had dinner together shortly after Theresa and Aaron's breakup."

Ava had to get her teeth unclenched before she could speak. "Again, you didn't think this was pertinent information in a murder investigation. I should have you charged with obstruction of justice."

"I didn't know any of this was important," Duran fired back. "Aaron's come in contact with a whole lot of people over the past twenty years, and I never met these women. They were merely names mentioned in a report that I would have skimmed."

The skimming was possibly true since Duran would have been looking for any red flags on Aaron, but that didn't mean the man hadn't used the connections to select his victims. After all, Duran could have reasoned that Aaron could have told Theresa about Aaron, and then Monica could have passed along the info to Sandy since the two women were friends.

"You're sure there's nothing in the PI reports about Monica Howell?" Harley asked Duran.

"Not that I can recall." Duran paused. "But I'll check."

"Do that. And, my advice if you find a connection, come clean, because right now, all this secrecy could land your butt in jail," Harley warned him.

"Where's Ava?" She heard someone call out.

She groaned because it was her father. "Edgar's here," she relayed to Duran.

"He's worried about you," Duran quickly supplied. "Tell him I'll call him as soon as I've finished the interview."

With that, Duran ended the call, and when her father called out her name again, she opened the interview room door and spotted Theo escorting Edgar toward her. Neither man looked pleased, but since Theo got a call, he handed Edgar off to her and stepped aside so he could answer his phone.

Edgar marched right into the interview room and slammed the door behind him. One look at him and Ava knew he was spitting mad, and it didn't take him long to jump right into the reason for that anger.

"Did you pressure the Austin cops into taking Duran into custody?" Edgar fired the question at them. "Do you have any idea what kind of publicity that's going to generate?"

So, no worry that his longtime friend could have tried his hand at attempted murder. No worry about her. But, yes, bad publicity would get Edgar revving.

"Consider this: Duran was in Austin at the time of the shooting," Harley explained before Ava could gear up to return verbal fire. "And not just in Austin but in the vicinity of the shooting. He could have been the one who tried to kill Ava. Was he firing those shots for you or because he was trying to cover up something he'd done?"

Judging from the way Edgar's shoulders snapped back, he hadn't been expecting that. "What the heck are you talking about?"

"Surveillance footage captured an image of Duran less than a block from the shooting," Ava provided. "And before you claim it's some kind of mistake, we just spoke to Duran and he admitted he was there."

"Why?" Edgar spat out.

"Because he got a report that Aaron was planning on seeing Caleb," Ava informed him.

She left it at that, letting Edgar fill in the blanks with possible answers, but Ava was going with the obvious on this. If Duran was telling the truth and hadn't attacked Harley and her, then he'd likely gone there to make sure Aaron and Caleb weren't about to expose Edgar and him for what they'd done twenty years earlier.

Edgar groaned and squeezed his eyes shut a moment. "Duran wouldn't shoot at you to stop a meeting like that. He would have found another way to handle it if there was any fallout from it."

Rather than come out and say she wasn't convinced of that at all, she gave him a flat look and went with the topic she'd just discussed with Duran. "Monica Howell, Theresa Darnell and Sandy Russo. If you've have any kind of contact, even of the second-hand variety, with any of those women, you need to tell us now. We're digging, and if we find out you've lied, the bad publicity will be the least of your worries."

Edgar cursed. "Those are the dead women, and I didn't know any of them." He seemed to be gearing up for a tirade, but he stopped and studied her. "Duran knew these women?"

"Two of them," she confirmed, causing Edgar to curse again.

Groaning, her father shook his head as if in disappointment or maybe disgust. "I didn't know. Now, you probably don't believe that, but it's the truth."

"Did you know about Duran paying Aaron blackmail money as recently as seven months ago?" Harley asked.

Edgar whipped his attention in Harley's direction, and either her father was putting on a good act or he truly hadn't known. "No," he said, his jaw muscles tightening and flexing. "But paying someone off doesn't mean Duran killed anyone.

Hell, if he'd wanted someone dead, he would have gone after Aaron."

Both Harley and she stared at Edgar, giving him some time to let that sink in. Maybe Duran hadn't taken the direct approach of going after Aaron.

"If Duran could set up Aaron for the murders," Harley spelled out, "Aaron would not have only gone to prison, he would have been totally discredited if he tried to tell anyone what had happened to him twenty years ago." He glanced at Ava. "And, if Ava isn't around to verify what Aaron says, then Duran, or the killer, could spin the truth any way he or she wants it spun."

Edgar stayed quiet for a long time and he finally shook his head again. "No, I won't believe Duran's behind this because that would mean he tried to kill you. He wouldn't have done that."

"The shooter missed," Harley reminded him.

More silence, but she saw the anger erupt in Edgar's eyes. "Duran didn't do this," he snarled, enunciating each word before he turned and threw open the door.

Her father took one step out into the hall, just one, before he smacked right into someone.

Caleb.

Chapter Eleven

Harley wasn't sure who was more shocked at the impromptu meeting. Ava, Caleb or Edgar. At the moment, he thought it might be a tie.

Figuring that Edgar might say something that would ignite a fierce backlash from Ava, Harley moved toward Caleb. Not that Harley would mind Ava doling out a verbal blast to her slimy father, but he didn't want Caleb caught up in any fallout. Neither would Ava, and she would end up regretting anything that could hurt Caleb.

"Caleb," Harley greeted, putting his hand on his shoulder to get him moving closer to Ava and him.

Caleb glanced at Ava. Then Edgar. Caleb definitely knew who the man was and, judging from the lack of friendly greeting in his expression, he was wary of his bio-grandfather.

Edgar stayed put in the hall, staring at Caleb as if his gaze had been pinned to him. Harley didn't see venom, just the shock. And maybe something else. Not love or affection but perhaps some kind of reckoning that he was face-to-face with his daughter's child. A child he'd forced Ava to give up.

"Uh, Senator Lawson," Caleb said by way of greeting before he looked at Ava. "Sorry about just showing up like this, but do you have a minute so we can talk? You, too," he added to Harley.

That caused Harley's gut to tighten. He hoped like the devil that someone hadn't tried to hurt Caleb. Ava was going through enough right now without her firstborn being in danger.

"Of course," she said. And there was definitely love and affection in her eyes. Also some worry. She glanced at her father. "Could you please shut the door on your way out?"

Edgar didn't dole out one of his classic glares. He cleared his throat and directed his comments to Caleb. "I hope you know everything that happened when you were born was in your best interest."

Harley couldn't stop himself from groaning, and he thought maybe Ava would return some not-so-friendly fire. She didn't, though, and neither did Caleb. The young man simply walked over to Edgar.

"Excuse us, please," he said. "It's important that I speak to Deputy Lawson and Ranger Ryland." Then Caleb eased the door shut in Edgar's face.

Again, Harley didn't know who was more surprised by that, and he half expected for Edgar to throw open the door and start bellowing about what he perceived to be an insult.

He didn't.

Maybe because the senator had won that surprise award this round and was too stunned to be his usual jackass self. Either that or he'd been crushed by the gesture. Harley doubted it was the latter, but it couldn't have felt good to be rejected by his grandson even if it was a grandchild Edgar hadn't wanted anywhere in his life.

Caleb turned back to Ava and his expression was filled with worry when he took out his phone and handed it to her. "Someone emailed those to me about an hour ago," he explained.

With plenty of worry flooding her own expression, Ava took the phone, and Harley went to her side to see the blank email. Well, blank for words anyway. But there were three attachments and, before Ava clicked on them, Harley knew what she was going to see.

The three murdered women.

In each of them, the posed women had garbage bags covering their bodies and were wearing the masks of Ava's face.

"That's you," Caleb said, his voice trembling.

"Your face, just like the one on the mannequin someone left for you."

She nodded, passed the phone to Harley, and she looked directly at Caleb. "I'm sorry someone sent you these. It must have been a shock to open them and see the bodies."

"It was a shock to see your face on the bodies," Caleb clarified. He groaned and shook his head. "This isn't a mannequin. These women are real. Were real," he amended. "And the killer put your face on them when he killed them."

Ava stayed calm and led him to one of the chairs. When Caleb didn't sit, she did, and that prompted him to take the chair next to her. Harley intended to hear anything else Caleb had to say, but he was also taking a closer look at the photos, looking for anything that could lead them to the person who'd done this. Harley also sent Theo, Ava and himself copies of the photos, and he wanted the lab to take a hard look at them as well.

"Are the Rangers still watching your place to make sure you're okay?" she asked Caleb.

He nodded. "I told the one on duty that I needed to come here and talk to you, and he gave me a ride. He's waiting out front."

"Good. Because I don't want you going anywhere alone, not until we catch the person responsible."

"You're taking precautions, right?" Caleb asked but didn't wait for an answer. He looked up at Harley. "You're making sure she stays safe?"

"I'm trying," he assured Caleb, and Harley dragged a chair over so he could sit across from them. "Ava's a cop, so it's a fine line between protecting her and not trusting her cop skills. She's very good at what she does," he tacked onto that, hoping it would make Caleb worry less than he obviously was. But maybe reassuring him about her safety wasn't possible.

Caleb nodded as if trying to process what he'd been told. "Is the senator involved in any of this?" He tipped his head to his phone as Harley handed it back to him.

"He's personally alibied for the nights of the murders," Harley explained. "And, even though he's not one of my favorite people, I don't believe he'd actually try to hurt Ava."

Caleb studied his expression and, after a few moments, seemed to accept what Harley had just said. "But the killer could be someone trying to get back at the senator by going after his daughter and her baby?"

Bingo. Hopefully, the killer wouldn't go after both of Edgar's grandchildren and would leave Caleb out of this.

"I guess you think I should have just handled

this over the phone," Caleb said a moment later. "I mean instead of coming to Silver Creek—"

"It's okay," Ava interrupted. "It's good to see you." She dragged in a long breath. "Even if I would have felt better if you'd just stayed put, where you'd be safe. I want you *safe*, Caleb," she emphasized in a murmur.

The emotion practically flew off those words, and Harley could see it in every bit of her expression. She was hurting with worry for the son she hadn't been able to keep.

Caleb held Ava's gaze for several moments and then glanced at her stomach. "Do you know if you're having a boy or a girl?"

"A girl," she said, smiling just a little.

Caleb smiled, too. "I hope you don't take this the wrong way, but I always wanted a sibling. A little late, I know," he added with a nervous chuckle. "When she's old enough, will you tell her who I am?"

"I will," Ava assured him.

Caleb nodded, as if pleased with that, and he stood. "I'd better be getting back to Austin, and I'll stay put. Promise."

Ava walked to the door with him. "Uh, when this investigation is over, maybe we can have lunch or something?" she suggested.

This time the smile made it to his eyes and he nodded. "Good. I'd like that."

He muttered a goodbye, but the moment Caleb opened the door, Harley heard a familiar voice. Not Edgar this time. But rather Aaron.

Apparently, this was going to be the day for awkward encounters, and Harley went out into the hall in case things turned bad. Aaron was indeed coming up the hall, and Theo was with him, no doubt taking the man to an interview room.

Aaron froze, his gaze zooming straight to Caleb's, and Harley could tell that he recognized his bio-son. Of course he did. In this day of social media, Aaron had likely seen many photos of the young man, and Harley recalled Aaron mentioning that Caleb and he had spoken on the phone after Caleb had learned of their DNA connection.

"Caleb," Aaron said on a rise of breath.

Caleb nodded but certainly didn't dole out any of the warmth that he had to Ava. Maybe because Caleb had picked up on the clues that Aaron was a suspect in not only the shooting but also the murders.

Aaron continued to look at Caleb for several moments before his gaze fired to Harley's, then to Ava's when she also stepped into the hall.

"You'd better not be interrogating Caleb," Aaron snapped.

"We're not," Ava assured him. "Caleb just came by to talk."

Aaron didn't seem the least bit convinced of

that, but Theo didn't give him a chance to press for any other info.

"In here," Theo ordered, opening the door of the interview room across the hall.

Aaron kept his gaze fastened to Caleb. "Will you be around for a while? If so, maybe we can talk when I'm done."

Caleb shook his head. "I was just leaving." He paused. "I'll call you soon." He repeated his goodbye and started walking toward the front of the building.

"I'll have the Ranger who drove Caleb here text me when Caleb's safely back at his apartment," Harley whispered to Ava, hoping that would ease some of the worry she was no doubt feeling about Caleb being out and about.

"Go in and wait," Theo told Aaron.

Aaron did, after he watched Caleb until he was out of sight. Then, on a heavy sigh, he turned to Ava. "Don't you dare try to turn him against me," Aaron warned her.

Now that was the voice of a man who could kill, but Ava didn't take the bait and verbally strike back at him. She just waited until Theo had Aaron inside the interview room. Then Theo shut the door and turned toward Ava.

"Are you okay?" Theo asked her.

She nodded. "Someone sent Caleb photos of the murdered women."

"Yeah. I was looking at the text Harley forwarded to me when Aaron came in for his interview. You'll send them to the Ranger lab?" Theo directed that question at Harley.

"I will," Harley verified. "What about the summary of the reports from the PI? Did you get those yet?"

"I did, and I just got an email update about five minutes ago. You were copied on it, so it'll be in your in-box."

"They found something?" Ava asked, sounding plenty hopeful.

"Something that doesn't look good for Aaron," Theo verified. "The PI was watching Aaron's place the night Christina died. She wasn't out partying or visiting friends. She was at the apartment she shared with Aaron. He was the only person who came and went during the hours leading up to her death."

Oh, yeah. That definitely didn't look good for Aaron. "Too bad the PI didn't spot Aaron actually buying drugs," Harley commented.

Theo made a sound of agreement. "On that particular night, the PI didn't start surveillance until Aaron arrived home. Still, I'll be able to use this to put some pressure on Aaron. If he admits to buying Christina the drugs that killed her, then that might cause him to break and admit to other things."

If so, then Theo might be able to make an arrest today, and even if that arrest wasn't for the murders, it would put one of their prime suspects behind bars where he wouldn't be able to come after Ava or anyone else.

"One more thing," Theo went on. "I'm trying to get the militia member, Lionel Henderson, in for an interview to find out about his explosives training and to ask him about his possible relationships with Marnie, Aaron and any of our victims. So far, though, he hasn't returned any of my calls and he wasn't home when I sent someone out to his place. His boss says he hasn't showed up for work in the past two days."

Ava groaned softly. "He could be on the run."

That'd be Harley's guess. If Lionel had gotten word that both Marnie and Aaron had been brought in for questioning, then he might have figured it was time to disappear rather than face law enforcement with questions about his training with explosives. It was entirely possible Lionel had had nothing to do with the murders directly, but he'd almost certainly be able to tell them who'd hired him.

"Considering Aaron's mood, why don't Harley and you observe the first part of the interview?" Theo suggested. "If you see something in his body language, or if he says something that I'm not picking up on, then you can come in and let me know."

That arrangement suited Harley just fine, and it would give Ava a chance to catch her breath. Theo would ask the necessary questions and it was likely he'd be able to get a lot more out of Aaron than Ava would. Considering the brief encounter Aaron had had with Ava in the hall, Caleb and their past would be playing into this.

Harley didn't ask Ava if she was okay when they went into the interview room, but he did touch her arm and rub it lightly. Just enough to let her know he was there. She winced a little, causing him to yank back his hand. Then her own hand went to her stomach.

"That was the strongest movement she's ever had," Ava muttered. "I've felt flutters before, but this felt like she turned over or something."

That sent a whole lot of alarm through him. "Is that normal? Is the baby all right?"

"It's normal," she assured him. "I don't think you'll be able to feel it yet."

Still, she took his hand and pressed it to her stomach. He didn't feel anything. Well, nothing physical anyway, but touching Ava this way definitely had to break down some personal barriers for her.

"Sorry," Ava added. "She's still now."

There might have been an awkward silence if

there'd actually been a chance for that, but just as Harley drew back his hand, Theo started the interview on the other side of the observation glass.

Theo recited the Miranda warning to Aaron again and jumped right into a key question.

"Why didn't you volunteer that you'd had a relationship with Theresa Darnell?" Theo demanded.

Clearly, Aaron hadn't been expecting that because he opened his mouth, closed it and then cursed. "Marnie told you. Of course she did. She wants to get back at me any way she can."

Theo stared at him. "Answer the question."

Aaron huffed. "I didn't tell you because I thought it would look bad that I'd been involved with her."

"It does look bad," Theo verified. "And it looks especially bad when you've been questioned by law enforcement and you didn't come clean. Did you kill her?" Theo added without so much as a pause.

"No," Aaron howled. "Of course not. I haven't killed anybody. Theresa and I hung out for a while, that's all, and when Christina and I got back together, Theresa didn't like it much. She had words with Marnie when she went looking for me."

Theo continued to level that lethal cop's stare

on Aaron. "How about Sandy Russo? Did you know her, too?"

"No." Aaron spewed off another round of profanity.

"Well, Theresa and she were friends," Theo said, maybe stretching the truth there. The women knew each other, but Harley wasn't sure they'd been actual friends. Still, a cop was allowed to outright lie during an interview. "Did both women rile you enough to make them targets?"

Aaron stood so fast that the chair he'd been sitting in went flying back. "That's it. I want a lawyer."

Theo nodded, tucked his small notepad back into his pocket. "Call one and we'll resume this interview." He started for the door then stopped. "Oh, and when your lawyer arrives, I'll be questioning you about some info I recently learned. Info that you're the one who supplied Christina the drugs that killed her. Mention that to your lawyer, why don't you?"

Aaron did more cursing, but the moment Theo was out of the room, the man began to pace as well. Clearly agitated, Aaron took out his phone and made a call. Since it was likely to a lawyer, Harley turned off the sound in the observation room.

A moment later, Theo opened the door and

peered in at them. "I figured I could push at least another button or two before he lawyered up."

"Good idea," Harley assured him, and then he spoke aloud what they were all thinking. "You don't have enough to hold Aaron."

Theo made a quick sound of agreement. "Not unless we can get something on the drug purchase."

"Then that's where I'll start digging," Ava assured him.

Theo stepped back as if to let her get started on that, but his phone rang. He tensed when he glanced at the screen and then answered it. Seconds later, the sickening dread washed over Theo's face.

"We're on our way," Theo said to the caller and he hung up. "That was the 9-1-1 dispatcher. There's been another murder."

Chapter Twelve

As Theo, Harley and she drove toward the latest crime scene, Ava tried to force herself to stay composed. Hard to do, though, with the emotions whipping through her. It was next to impossible since those emotions were mixed with the adrenaline roller coaster that she'd been on for weeks now, the pregnancy hormones and the sickening dread of another murder.

Mercy, another dead woman.

Well, maybe it was. It could be another mannequin, but the witness had been certain it was a body.

That was all Theo, Harley and she knew at this point. The teenage witness who'd been at the creek to take a swim had seen the body of a woman lying on the creek bank and had called 9-1-1. Other than the location and that it appeared the woman had a trash bag on her, the dispatcher hadn't been able to get much else out of him because the boy was in shock.

Like Theo and Harley, Ava kept watch around them as Theo drove away from town and toward the creek that had given the town its name. The creek coiled through the surrounding area ranches and was accessible by road at three different points. This location would be the most remote of the three since there were no houses nearby. That was no doubt why the killer had chosen it for a body dump.

"I'd rather you wait in the cruiser," Theo said to her when he pulled to a stop on the narrow road near the bridge.

She glanced over at Harley who was in the backseat, and Ava knew he wanted the same thing. For her to remain in the relative safety of the cruiser. It was tempting to do just that.

It was also impossible.

She was a cop, and she was the cause of the murders. Yes, she would take precautions and had done so by wearing a Kevlar vest, but no precaution would completely ensure her safety. It was the same for Theo and Harley.

"I'll be careful," was all she said.

Ava ignored Harley's heavy sigh and looked around to begin her assessment of the crime scene.

Other than the remote location, she could see why the killer had chosen this spot for a body dump. There was no steep incline leading down to the creek. The killer could have stopped near where they were now and dragged or carried the body to the creek bank.

Posing wouldn't have taken long, less than a minute if the garbage bag and mask had already been in place. A quick in-and-out where he or she obviously hadn't been spotted or someone would have reported it.

Ava saw a lanky teenage boy in shorts and a tee, sitting on the bridge railing. The witness, no doubt, and he was visibly shaken. His bike was lying on its side near him, and he had turned himself away from the creek. He had his arms folded over his chest and was crying. Ava didn't know his name, but she knew the boy's parents, David and Melanie Buckner, who owned a ranch just up the road. Since the couple both worked in town, they'd no doubt be here soon.

Theo sighed, too, at Ava's insistence that she not stay put, and he opened his door just as a second cruiser came to a stop behind them. Deputies Jesse Ryland and Nelline Rucker got out, immediately heading for Theo's cruiser. Both Harley and Ava stepped out.

"You know the boy?" Theo asked Jesse. He took a pair of evidence gloves from the cruiser but left the door open. No doubt so they could dive back in if necessary. Ava and Harley did the same.

Jesse nodded. "Eli Buckner. His folks bought a horse from me for his fourteenth birthday. You want me to see to him?"

"Yeah," Theo verified. "Get him into your cruiser so if there's any evidence on the bridge, it won't be stepped on when his folks get here. Also, I want him away from any potential trouble." He turned to Nelline. "Wait here and keep watch to make sure we're not about to be ambushed."

Even though Nelline was a veteran cop, that put a whole lot of concern in her eyes, and she automatically moved her hand to the butt of her weapon. "You want me to go ahead and call the CSIs and medical examiner?" she asked.

Theo shook his head. "I want to verify that it is indeed a body before we get all of that rolling. Still, try to preserve the scene as best you can." He motioned for Harley and Ava to follow him.

All three kept watch around them, but they also checked the ground for any signs of what had happened here. There were no actual drag marks as there had been at the scene of the last murder, but the ground appeared to have been trampled in spots. They avoided those spots, just in case the CSIs could recover shoe prints, and made their way to the creek bank.

Normally, this was a serene location with the sound of the water rushing over the rocks, the spring breeze gently stirring the leaves on the trees and the wildflowers dotting the landscape. But there was nothing serene about the woman lying just ahead. One look at her and Ava knew this wasn't a hoax.

This was indeed another murder.

The woman's body was posed exactly as the others and had the mask of Ava's face. Even though this was the fourth time Ava had seen the mask on a victim, it still gave her that over-whelming crush of grief and guilt.

Ava drew her gun and whirled around when a dark blue truck came screeching to a halt behind the cruisers. But it wasn't the killer. It was Eli's parents, and they both immediately barreled out of the vehicle and started running toward their son as Jesse was leading the boy to the cruiser.

She didn't put her gun back in the holster. Ava kept a two-handed grip on it, pointing it down but knowing it'd be ready, and they approached the body.

The dead woman's hair was the same color as Ava's. That was about the only part of her they could see what with the mask and the garbage bag. Theo gloved up while Harley took some photos of the body, and then, using extreme cau-tion so as to touch as little as possible, Theo lifted the corner of the mask.

"I know her," Ava blurted out. Her voice was

strained because of the fresh slam of adrenaline, but even with the shock of seeing that face, she knew this was not the killer's usual MO. "She's an investigative reporter, Lacey George. She works for one of the San Antonio newspapers."

All the other victims had lived closer to Silver Creek, and none had been from a large city. Ava had no idea if Lacey fit the profile of the other victims by having or losing a child, but she was well aware of the woman's connection to at least one of their suspects.

"Years ago, Lacey had some run-ins with my father about his policies," Ava added. "Which means she had run-ins with Duran."

And that obvious connection had her mentally stopping to consider what this might mean.

Duran likely wouldn't have murdered someone with such an immediate link to him unless this was some kind of reverse psychology. If so, then he might have thought he could eliminate someone who'd been a pain to Edgar and him while pushing his agenda to torment her. Maybe with the end game to kill her or drive her mad.

Theo eased the mask back in place and took out his phone to call in the CSIs and the medical examiner. Harley took out his phone as well, and a moment later, Ava realized that was so he could run a background check on the dead woman.

While they did that, Ava glanced around, first

looking for any signs of explosives or someone who might be lurking and ready to attack them. She didn't see either of those things. However, since the body was close to water, she stepped around Harley and looked down at the soft, damp dirt on the narrow bank.

"Maybe a shoe print," she pointed out when she saw the indentation.

Theo and Harley continued their phone conversations, but both of them leaned in to have a closer look. "Nelline," Theo called out to the deputy. "I need an evidence marker down here and steer away from the section of the grass that's been trampled. Follow in our footsteps."

The marker was a flag that would alert anyone to the possible evidence and prevent someone from stepping onto it and destroying it. If they got lucky, there might be enough of an impression for the CSIs to determine the shoe size and type of footwear, and that could maybe help them narrow down their suspects.

While Nelline hurried to Theo with the marker, Ava continued to look around, moving slowly and cautiously, scanning the ground for anything.

"Lacey George," Harley said, obviously relaying what he'd just learned about their dead woman. "She's thirty-six, an investigative reporter for Fulbright Media. Divorced. She has a son who's fourteen, but her ex has full custody of the child."

So that was a deviation, too, of sorts. "Had she been reported missing?" Ava asked.

"Only about a half hour ago. That's why we haven't gotten the alert yet. She lives alone, and her boss reported her as missing when she didn't show up for work and he couldn't contact her. He hadn't seen her since she'd left her office the previous afternoon."

That was a large gap of time, more than twenty-four hours, and it meant any of their suspects could have taken Lacey, killed her and posed her here. The posing likely would have happened at night, but none of their suspects had been in custody or in interviews then.

"Since she's a reporter, the killer could have lured her out with the possibility of a story," Ava commented.

That kept all of their suspects in the running. An investigative reporter likely would have met any of the three if promised juicy details about the murders.

"I requested a thorough background check on her," Harley explained, putting away his phone. "The Rangers will try to pin down anyone who might have seen her so we can figure out how and where she was taken."

So far, knowing those things hadn't helped

them catch this killer, Ava had to hang on to the hope that this time it would be different. This time, there had to be an eyewitness or some surveillance camera footage. That footage had been a long shot with the women taken in or around Silver Creek, but a city the size of San Antonio had plenty of operating cameras.

"Take a quick look around, and then we'll head back to the cruiser," Theo instructed while he started snapping some photos as well.

Ava didn't balk at having to leave the scene. Now that they had verified there was a body and had gotten a preliminary ID, there wasn't much more they could do other than secure the scene and wait for the CSI team to arrive.

Harley moved closer to the creek, peering down into the water, maybe looking to see if anything had inadvertently been dropped in there. It was another of those things that needed to be checked. If something was there, it'd need to be secured in case the water swept it away before the CSIs could retrieve it.

Ava scanned the trees that were on the bank just upstream. One of the bigger oaks had a rope swing tied to it, and the underbrush around it had been tamped down. She didn't think that was a recent occurrence though. It looked like that specific spot got plenty of use.

The area to the right of the rope swing, though,

was congested with trees of varying sizes, weeds and vines. The trees were thicker here, so not much of the sunlight was making its way through, but she still saw something that caught her eye.

Something that had Ava's stomach dropping to her knees.

Because there was something on the ground that didn't look as if it was part of the natural landscape. It looked more like green camos.

"I think there's another body," she said, motioning to some underbrush about ten yards away from where she was standing.

She took one step closer to get a better look and she felt something brush over the top of her boot. Harley must have seen or heard something because he practically lunged at her. He turned her, sheltering her body with his just as he'd done when the shots had been fired at them. But this was no shot. No.

It was an explosion.

HARLEY HAD SEEN the glint of the thin wire that had nearly been concealed with leaves, and he knew instantly what it was. A trip wire no doubt connected to an explosive device.

He didn't have time to shout. Didn't have time to do much of anything except grab Ava and pull her to the ground, all the while praying that would be enough to save her and the baby.

The blast was deafening, and it shot out debris, pelting his back and legs. Harley felt the sting of the impact but not actual pain. Thank God. Maybe it was the same for Ava.

He waited long gut-wrenching moments to make sure there wasn't a second blast, and when there wasn't, he lifted himself off Ava enough to check her. She was a little pale and definitely shaken up, but he couldn't see any visible injuries. That was one prayer answered, but Harley knew they weren't out of danger just yet.

"Are you okay?" he asked just as Theo called out the same question to them. The sheriff, having hit the ground, too, was only a few feet away from the dead woman.

"I'm not hurt," Ava assured both of them. "I didn't land on my stomach. Harley cushioned the blow."

When he replayed those nightmarish moments in his head, and he would do just that, he'd wish he had gotten to her before she'd tripped the wire. That might have saved her the terror of the blast along with not destroying the hell out of their crime scene. Right now, it was littered with leaves and bits of shrubs and tree bark that had gone flying during the impact.

On the road, Harley could hear the flurry of

activity. Both Jesse and Nelline had obviously gotten out of the cruiser, but he was hoping their witness and his parents hadn't remained on scene. No need for them to see any of this, not when they were already going to have to deal with enough.

"Do you see any other trip wires or devices?" Theo called out to no one in particular. He was certainly checking the ground for both items.

"No," Jesse answered. "There appears to be a body though."

"Yes," Ava verified. "That's where I was heading when I triggered a bomb." She groaned and Harley could hear the dread and apology in that simple sound.

"Not your fault," Harley reminded her. "This is the sick SOB's doing."

"There might be something by Harley's right foot," Nelline shouted. He glanced up to see the deputy surveilling the area with binoculars. Then Harley looked at his boot.

And he cursed.

Because, undeniably, there was a thin silver wire there. Just inches from him, and he didn't know where either end of it was. If he moved, he could set it off.

"The bomb squad's on the way," Jesse relayed a moment later. "No one move. I'll get another pair of binoculars and see if I can figure out a safe path to get you out of there."

This definitely wasn't an ideal situation, but it was a best-case scenario for the killer. Theo, Ava and he were pinned down, unable to move. Heck, even lifting their weapons to defend themselves could get them all killed. Yeah, definitely not ideal. Because at this moment, the killer could be getting in position to gun them down.

Beneath him, he could feel Ava's body. Her muscles were tight and knotted, and she was clearly trying to steady her breathing. Hard to do, though, when they were facing death. Harley knew she wasn't nearly as worried for herself as she was for the baby, and he cursed the killer for putting their child in this kind of danger.

"I see another wire," Nelline called out. "It's on the creek bank by the tree with the tire swing."

That'd been the exact spot Harley had been heading when he'd caught a glimpse of the wire from the corner of his eye. If he'd gone there, he could have ended up blowing them all to smithereens since he'd had no idea how powerful the explosives were. He doubted, though, that there were decoys. No. The killer likely intended for this to be their final resting place. It wouldn't fit with his MO, but it could be the big finale to the four murders that had already been committed.

Correction: five murders.

Because that body in the woods had to be connected to what was happening now. Maybe another dead woman meant to lure one of them into the wooded area where they'd trip a wire.

"There's another wire," Jesse let them know. "Theo, you might not be able to see it, but it's by the rock at the top of your head. It seems to lead to the—" He stopped and cursed. "The bridge. I'll move the cruiser with Eli and his folks."

Yes, and it was more than a precaution since the blast could not only reach the cruiser, it could end up hurting or killing those inside.

"Nelline," Theo called out again. "Make sure we don't have any snipers trying to get into position to shoot us."

Ava didn't react to that. No doubt because it had already occurred to her that they were basically sitting ducks.

Harley hated not being able to stop anything bad from happening to her. He hated this smothering sense of dread that was pulsing through him. But he forced his heartbeat to calm some so he could stop it from throbbing in his ears. He needed to be able to hear in case someone was trying to sneak up on them.

The air felt so still that it seemed to be holding its breath, waiting. Bracing. Theo's body was doing the same, and he figured Ava was having a similar reaction. Along with cursing the monster who'd put them in this position so they weren't able to keep their child safe.

"There's a timer," Nelline shouted. "Oh, God. It's on the one by the tire swing. Theo, it's ticking down."

"How much time?" Theo asked.

"One minute and thirty seconds," Nelline answered, her voice strained to the hilt.

Harley didn't waste his breath on the profanity that he wanted to snarl. It wouldn't help. Right now, he had to focus, to figure out the lowest level of risk to get Ava out of there.

He lifted his head, glancing around them. "Other than the wire by my boot, are there any others near Ava and me?" Harley asked.

Precious seconds crawled by while he waited for Jesse and Nelline to check the area. Seconds that he could practically see ticking off on that damn timer.

"I can't see any," Nelline finally answered.

Not exactly a resounding no, but he couldn't expect the deputies to be able to see through them and the debris to locate trigger wires.

"Check the ground that leads from here to the road," Harley instructed the deputies.

He was almost positive he could retrace the route Ava, Theo and he had taken to get from the cruiser to the body, and they hadn't set off any devices on the walk down. Still, that could have been pure luck, and a fraction of an inch could be the difference between living and dying.

While that ate up even more seconds with the deputies checking, Harley helped Ava to her feet. They both stayed low, both searching the area around them. Across from them, Theo was doing the same thing.

"I can't see anything," Nelline finally said. "You need to move now. There's less than a minute left on the timer."

That revved up his heartbeat even higher and Harley took hold of Ava's arm with his left hand while he tried to keep his gun ready in his right. A thousand thoughts went through his head. Bad thoughts. Thoughts of how he wished he had done a whole lot of things differently so Ava and his baby wouldn't be here right now.

Ava fired glances all around them as she moved. Fast. He was thankful she was in such good shape because even though she had to be terrified for the baby, she moved like the cop that she was. Fast and steady. Keeping watch of every step they took to make sure it wasn't their last.

It seemed to take a lifetime or two to reach the road, and the moment their feet were on the pavement, they hurried to the open doors of the cruiser.

Behind them, the woods exploded in a fireball.

Chapter Thirteen

While Harley drove toward her house, Ava tried to force her body to level out even though that was impossible. Not with the vivid memories of lying on that ground, knowing that every breath she took could be her last.

In those moments, she'd gone through an emotional gambit of cursing herself for being there. Cursing the killer for putting them all in danger and for murdering a woman for the sole purpose of trying to lure them to their deaths. But Ava had also prayed that her baby would come out of this unscathed.

That prayer had been answered.

After everyone had gotten clear of the explosions, Theo and Harley had driven her straight to the hospital to make sure the baby was okay. She was. So were Theo, Harley, her and everyone else who'd been near the series of blasts. That was somewhat of a miracle and probably not at all what the killer had intended. He or she had likely planned on multiple deaths to add to the two that had already been on scene.

No one had been able to get close enough to the body in the shrubs to determine who he or she was, but that was yet another thing that'd need to be checked. An ID could give them yet another clue about the killer.

Now that Harley had dropped Theo off at the sheriff's office so he could assemble the team needed to investigate the blast site and interview the teenager who'd found the first body, Harley and she would soon be at her place. It'd been where Theo had ordered her to go and get some rest.

Of course, rest was impossible, what with her mind racing and every nerve in her body on edge. Still, she hadn't had the fight in her to try to convince him to let her stay and help.

Harley hadn't pushed her either way. In fact, he was mostly silent, doling out a few worried looks, but he hadn't mentioned that, because of her pregnancy she should be on desk duty and not out in the field. He hadn't blamed her for anything that'd happened.

But Ava was blaming herself.

"If I'd just dug harder after the first murder, we might have caught the killer by now," she muttered and instantly regretted that had come out of her mouth. "I didn't narrow down the suspects until Monica's death, and by then it was too late."

Harley shot her one of those flat looks as he pulled into the garage at her house. "You did everything you could have done. Theo and the other deputies, too. Even the mayor called me in to help. Yeah, he did it because he was trying to cut back on the bad publicity, but he assisted with covering all the bases by getting Theo and you the extra help you needed so we stood the best chance possible of catching this SOB."

So, she'd gotten a lecture after all, though not the one about her being out in the field. And every word he'd said was true. Still, the truth hadn't helped any of the victims, and so far, it hadn't helped anyone else who was in this killer's path.

As they'd done previously, Harley and she checked the house and, once they were sure it was clear, Ava immediately excused herself to go take a shower. She needed a moment to gather herself, and resting was out. Instead, Ava was hoping a warm shower would clear her head enough so she could get on her laptop and help with the investigation in any way she could.

With a crime scene in disarray, it would take the CSIs days to process it, and they wouldn't even be let into the area until the bomb squad had done its thing. They'd need to make sure there weren't other devices and collect the pieces of the explosives so they could be sent to the crime lab. The entire process could take a lot longer than they had. The killer was clearly escalating, and there was no telling where he'd strike next or what he would do.

After she stepped from the shower, she groaned softly when she caught a glimpse of herself in the mirror. She looked as if she'd been through the wringer—which she had. But since she didn't want to cause Harley to worry any more than he already was, she combed her wet hair, put on a pair of loose pajamas and tried to look as composed as she possibly could when she went back into the kitchen.

She instantly smelled the chicken noodle soup and saw that Harley had been busy while she'd showered. He'd fixed the soup, a couple of grilled cheese sandwiches and had poured two glasses of juice and another of milk.

Ava had to smile. "You're taking care of me."

"Trying to," he said, returning the smile. A smile that didn't make it to his eyes because of the worry she'd known would be there.

"Any word from Theo yet?" she asked while she drank some of the juice.

"Yeah. He texted a couple of minutes ago to let us know that he'd just received a report that

Lionel Henderson, the explosives expert we've been looking for, has been reported missing."

"For how long?" she asked.

"No one has seen him since yesterday morning. The Rangers pinged his phone, and it's apparently on the side of the road less than a quarter of a mile from the area of the creek where the explosives went off." He paused a heartbeat. "The other body in the woods was probably his."

She knew it couldn't be a coincidence that the explosives expert had ended up that close to the crime scene for their latest victim. A crime scene where there'd been multiple explosives. Ava had to guess that Lionel had assisted the killer, and then the killer had considered him too much of a liability to continue breathing.

"Five dead bodies," she muttered. "Maybe more."

"Yeah," he agreed.

Ava set down her juice and looked at him. "Just let me say this. I'm sorry. Sorry for believing you'd cut a deal for my father. Sorry that I've put you in the middle of this. The killer wouldn't have come after you had—"

She stopped, had to, because he went to her, pulled her into his arms and kissed her. Not a reassuring peck either. A full-blown kiss with his mouth pressing hard against hers. There was a lot of emotion.

A lot of heat as well.

But Ava figured this kiss wasn't about heat. Harley had probably used it to shut down something he hadn't wanted her to say. And it was working. Working, too, because of that heat it was churning out. Hard to keep thinking about killers and such when Harley's mouth triggered a whole other set of emotions in her.

She felt some of the tension drain from her body and everything inside her went a little slack. An amazing feeling considering that, just moments earlier, every nerve in her body had been firing on all cylinders. The nerves were still firing but in a whole different way. One that reminded her that, despite everything, she was still hotly attracted to this man who'd once been her lover.

Harley finally pulled back and she instantly felt the loss of the heat. A small sound of protest left her mouth before she could stop it.

"I'm not going to apologize for that," he drawled.

"Good." Because she didn't want an apology. Ava wanted another kiss, so that's what she got.

She took hold of Harley's arm. Tugging him back to her and pressing herself against him, she kissed him. Yes, it skyrocketed the heat, but she no longer felt on the verge of falling apart.

The kiss was way too hard and hungry for

something meant to comfort, and every inch of her responded. She'd done this with Harley before, kissed him until her legs had gone weak, and her body seemed to know what was coming. And what was coming was more.

Well, if she didn't stop it, that is.

Ava didn't want to stop it. Not yet anyway. Maybe not ever. She just took and took, deepening the kiss until she got the full taste of him.

Her body recalled that taste, too, and the feel of Harley's hand when he skimmed it down her back, urging her to move even closer to him. She did. Until her breasts were pressed against the hard muscles in his chest. That upped the heat even more, and she responded by taking hold of his jaw so she could do with his mouth exactly what she pleased.

A husky sound of arousal came from deep within his throat and he apparently was after some pleasing, too, because while he kissed her senseless, his skimming hand went lower and lower. He cupped her butt, pressing her so that she was right against his erection.

Ava upped the ante, too, and she lowered her mouth to his neck, trailing her tongue from the base of his ear to his throat. He groaned, cursed her and then stepped back.

His breath was gusting now. So was hers. And the heat was there in his eyes as he stared at her. She could sense his arousal in every part of her. But she could sense his hesitation, too, and, for one horrible moment, she thought he might say that this had to stop, that the timing was all wrong.

And it was.

But that didn't mean they had to stop. It didn't mean they had to try to work out what this might mean. Not right now anyway. Later, there'd be a price to pay for her seeking comfort in Harley's arms, but "not right now" seemed an eternity away.

Ava kissed him again and had no plans to stop.

HARLEY HAD GOTTEN so caught up in the heat of Ava's kiss that he'd forgotten one big important point.

That Ava was pregnant.

But he sure as heck remembered it when he felt things start to escalate. A big-time escalation since she was adding some touching to the kisses. Her hand was wandering down the front of his shirt and heading to his jeans.

That was the trouble with them being former lovers. The heat spiked a whole lot sooner than if they'd just been making out for the first time. And his body was pressuring him to keep spiking the heat, to keep letting her hand move to his jeans while he moved them both to the bedroom.

However, the pregnancy could be a game changer.

It wasn't easy, but he pulled back to meet her eyes and hoped he had enough air in his lungs to speak. Man, she was beautiful. Always had been. But now her face was flushed with arousal and her eyes were filled with hunger for him. He was sure that same hunger for her was in his eyes, too, but he needed to get some things straight.

"I figure it's okay for a pregnant woman to have sex," he threw out there. "If not, there'd be a lot of frustrated people in the world. But I need to make sure you're okay with it."

She blinked as if she, too, had just remembered the baby, despite the baby bump pressing between them right now. Ava paused, but he wasn't sure if that was because she was considering what he'd said or if, like him, she was just trying to gather her breath.

It was the latter.

Ava confirmed that when she muttered, "I'm sure," a split second before she slid her hand around the back of his neck and pulled him to her.

The heat was instant, returning with a vengeance that upped the need even more. Something Harley hadn't thought possible since he was already burning for her.

He slid his arms around her, returning the kiss

while she backed him in the direction of the bedroom. This was definitely familiar ground. When they'd been lovers, they'd made this trek, often discarding clothes along the way because they hadn't been able to wait to get their hands on each other.

That happened now, too.

The hunger and need were there, already clawing away at them, and it didn't surprise him when Ava paused the kissing only long enough to unbutton his shirt and rid him of it and his holster. Harley caught onto that, hooking it around his arm because even with all this intense heat, he knew he needed to keep his weapon nearby.

She immediately went after his chest, landing some well-placed kisses there that ate away at what little self-control he had. Harley had to battle not to pull her to the floor then and there.

Thankfully, her pajama top was loose and silky, and he managed to get it off her as well. Then, he eased her against the wall, anchoring her there while he shoved down the cups of her bra and kissed her nipples. She made the exact sound he wanted to hear. A silky moan.

Her body went a little slack for a moment as she gave in to the pleasure of him kissing her. But only a moment. Before her own leash on her self-control stopped, and she got them moving again.

Into the bedroom.

And toward the bed.

She took his mouth while she fumbled with his belt buckle. Ava kept brushing her fingers against his erection, causing his body to start begging for release. Since that couldn't happen, not yet anyway, he took matters into his own hands. He yanked off his belt and worked his way out of his boots, jeans and boxers before he put down his holster and gun. Then, he tackled getting Ava's pajama bottoms off. They were as loose as her top and practically slid from her body.

That's when Harley got an eyeful.

Her breasts were full, rising high against her bra that he'd shoved down. As always, her body was perfect. Yeah, especially with the baby bump.

He took a moment to lean down and kiss her stomach. Then he trailed a few kisses lower to the front of her panties. Her breath caught again. She made that silky sound of pleasure and caught onto his hair to anchor herself.

Even though his body was urging him to take her now, he still continued the kisses, letting the pleasure of it roll right through both of them.

"Now," she insisted when she obviously could take no more.

She pushed him back onto the bed, following on top of him, and she gave him a deep, long kiss while she got rid of her panties.

The curtains were closed, and they hadn't turned on the lights, but there was enough illumination coming from the open bathroom door that he had no trouble seeing her.

Watching her as she straddled him.

Going at a slow, almost torturous pace, she took him inside her. Inch by inch. And she kept her eyes closed until she had all of him. Then she opened them and met his gaze.

Amazing.

And he didn't think he felt that way about her simply because of the sex. No. He'd never felt this much intensity with anyone as he had with Ava.

She began to move, starting the strokes that immediately caused the heat and pleasure to spike. He latched onto her hips, not that she needed help but just so he could touch her, so he could experience the way she felt beneath his hands.

The strokes got faster. Harder. Deeper. Until everything began to pinpoint to fulfilling this clawing need that would not be denied. Until he felt the climax ripple through her.

And only then did Harley let go.

Chapter Fourteen

Ava woke with a jolt and it took her a moment to realize she wasn't alone. That Harley was holding her.

And he was naked.

She was naked as well, and it took her another moment to realize this wasn't some dream from the past. It was the real deal. A hot, naked cowboy. Hot, amazing sex, and it'd obviously worn her out enough that she was able to fall asleep. That was somewhat of a miracle, considering the events of the past few days.

He wasn't asleep though. She looked over at him to see that he was not only wide awake but that he was still taking care of her. He'd draped the quilt over her, had her snuggled in his arms, and was almost certainly keeping watch. Guarding her. He'd moved his holster and gun to the nightstand where it'd be in easy reach.

That was a jolting reminder of the danger.

And that led to reminders of what had happened between them.

Ava didn't groan, but she knew this was the time of reckoning. Now that her body was sated and the pleasure buzz was fading, she needed to deal with what this all meant. Quickly deal with it and then get back to work.

"How long have I been asleep?" she asked.

"About an hour. Not long enough." He leaned in and kissed her, igniting the pleasure buzz again and making her want to sink right back into him. She absolutely couldn't do that though.

"I have to find my phone and check for updates from Theo," she insisted. Her phone hadn't rung or dinged with a text, Ava was certain she would have heard that, but it was possible Theo or someone else had sent an important email.

Harley reached over onto the side of the bed and produced her phone. His, too. "I've been checking," he assured her. "Nothing's come in."

She glanced at the time on her phone and did groan now. It was already past 6:00 p.m., and while she'd clearly needed the rest, that would no doubt mess up any chance of her getting a good night's sleep. Then again, the killer had already ruined that possibility. She hadn't slept well since the murders had started.

"It'll be dark soon," Harley pointed out. "The bomb squad will still be on scene but will have to shut down for the night. It might be morning before anyone can get to the body to verify that it's Lionel Henderson."

Ava had suspected as much. "But they're sure it's a body?" she asked. "I mean, there's no chance the person was just unconscious? Or another mannequin?"

"No chance," Harley verified. "When I spoke to Theo earlier, while you were in the shower, he said he'd gotten an initial report that there'd been massive damage in the spot where the body had been."

In other words, if the person had been alive, he would have died in the blasts. She doubted, though, that the killer would have left the explosives expert alive and waiting to be blown up. No. The killer couldn't have risked Lionel being able to tell them anything about who'd hired him.

"Are you okay?" he asked.

She was pretty sure that not-so-simple question involved both her and the baby. "We're fine," she assured him, not addressing the other part of that simple question. The part about how she was dealing emotionally with what had just happened between them.

"Good," he said, obviously willing to accept her answer. He brushed a soft kiss on her mouth that still managed to pack a lot of heat. "We'll talk once things have settled down."

That was about the best offer he could have made. Harley wasn't going to pressure her into trying to figure out what any of this meant, which also meant they were on the same mental page. Then again, the danger had a way of putting everything else on hold.

After yet another of those heat-packing kisses, he caused her to mentally groan when he moved away and sat up. "You should probably eat something, and I need to grab a shower. After that, we could keep going through the PI reports to see if there's anything in them to link us to the killer."

It was another good offer, and Ava knew he was right about her needing to eat. Just because they had a killer to catch, it didn't mean she could neglect anything to do with the baby.

She got the cheap thrill of seeing a naked Harley head to the shower. Mercy, the man was built, and just seeing him fired up more than it should.

"Eat and work," she muttered, reminding her body that it had already had all it was going to get of Harley tonight.

While Harley showered, Ava dressed and, bringing both her phone and gun with her, she made her way into the kitchen. She checked out the windows, looking for any signs of trouble, but both her front and back yards were empty. Added to that, two of her neighbors who'd been out walking their dogs had stopped to chat on the sidewalk just across the street. Since everyone in Silver Creek knew about the murders, one of them would have alerted her had they seen anything suspicious.

Well, they would if they actually saw it.

She thought of the mannequin's head that the killer had managed to put on her back porch. Way too close for comfort, but it was still light out right now, so that added a small level of safety. However, as Harley had pointed out, it'd be dark soon and the killer might make his next move. That was the reason Ava moved away from the window.

The soup and grilled cheese that Harley had made were now stone-cold, but since she didn't want to cook anything else, she heated them up, poured herself another glass of milk and carried her plate to the table so she could boot up her laptop. She hadn't even managed to open the file on the PI reports when Harley came in.

Dressed, and with his hair damp from his shower, he looked far better than any man should. And her expression must have let him know exactly what she was thinking because the corner of his mouth lifted in a smile.

"You have that same effect on me," Harley assured her in that hot drawl that caused her body to go all warm again. She was fighting the urge to get up and kiss him when his phone rang.

His smile faded and Harley tensed as he glanced at the screen. "It's Quentin Dalton, the Ranger who's watching Caleb."

Ava practically rocketed to her feet, and the alarm shot through her. Oh, God. Had something happened to Caleb?

She didn't have to ask Harley to put the call on speaker. He did, and she immediately heard the Ranger's voice pour through the room. It was a voice she recognized because she recalled meeting Quentin a time or two when Harley and she had still been together.

"Caleb hasn't been hurt or anything like that," Quentin immediately said, no doubt to give them some reassurance, but Ava wasn't reassured of anything. Just the fact the Ranger had called meant there was a problem of some kind.

"What happened?" Harley asked, taking the words right out of her mouth.

"Caleb got spooked, and he wants to see Ava and you. I'm driving him to your place now."

"What?" Ava couldn't say fast enough. "Why? What happened?"

"Someone hacked his social media accounts and posted pictures of the dead women." Quentin's response was equally fast.

"There was a warning from the hacker that you were next," Caleb added. His voice was a tangle of nerves. "That the killer was coming for you tonight."

"Hell," Harley grumbled. "You've reported it?" he asked Quentin.

"Oh, yeah, and the lab folks will be looking into the hacking. I told Caleb that, but I couldn't talk him out of coming to see you."

"He couldn't," she heard Caleb verify. "I just didn't want to be in that apartment when I knew what the killer had planned. God, he put your face on those women he killed. He said he was going to kill you *tonight*," Caleb emphasized. "I couldn't just sit still and do nothing."

Ava wanted to demand that Caleb go back to his apartment. Because she knew full well the hacking could have been meant to get Caleb to do exactly this. Leave the relative safety of his apartment and go out on the road where the killer would have an easier time getting to him.

A killer who would use her son to hurt her in the worst possible way.

"Where are you right now?" Harley asked, sounding calm, but Ava could see the urgency and intensity in his expression.

"About fifteen miles from Silver Creek," Quentin answered. "I'm turning off the interstate now. And, yeah, I know this trip isn't smart, but I want to get to Ava's place before dark."

"Don't blame Ranger Dalton," Caleb insisted.

"I told him I was coming to Silver Creek one way or another. I didn't want him to call you until we were closer because I was afraid you'd convince him to turn around and take me back to Austin."

Ava shook her head but didn't press Caleb about what he thought he could do to stop a killer from coming after her. Obviously, he believed he could protect her in some way and, while that touched her, she was also worried about his safety. She was a cop. Caleb wasn't.

"I'm going to call the sheriff and see if he can spare a deputy to go out to meet you and finish escorting you here," Ava insisted.

Since there was only one road leading to Silver Creek from the interstate, she didn't have to guess which route Quentin would be taking, and she picked up her phone to make the call to Theo. Before she could press the number, she heard a sound she didn't want to hear.

Quentin cursed.

Just a single word of raw profanity, followed by something else that had her heart dropping to her knees.

The sickening boom of a car crash.

HARLEY HAD ALREADY braced himself for something bad happening, but he'd been praying that his gut was wrong. That Quentin and Caleb would be able to make it to Silver Creek without incident so that Caleb would be safe.

But that clearly wasn't the case.

There was the distinctive sound of metal crashing into metal. And, mixed with that horrible noise, were the moans that followed.

"Caleb?" Ava blurted out. There was absolute terror in her voice now. "Are you all right?"

The only answer she got were more moans, and that was enough to get Ava moving. She was already dressed, but she grabbed her holster and made the call to Theo. Since Harley knew there was no way he could talk her out of going to the scene, he strapped on his own holster and Kevlar vest. He had her put on a vest, too, before they hurried to the garage.

"Quentin?" Harley pressed, shifting the call to hands-free so he could focus on the drive.

Still nothing other than more of those moans.

"They're alive," Harley reminded Ava, "and Quentin's vehicle would have had airbags."

No need for him to spell out, though, that it wouldn't be bullet-resistant like their cruiser, meaning Caleb and Quentin could be in big trouble right now. Because the odds were this wasn't just an accident.

That sent Harley's mind spinning with all sorts of bad scenarios. Of the killer running Quentin and Caleb off the road so he could get to them.

Maybe not to kill them right off, either, but to use Caleb to get to Ava.

It twisted at Harley to think it might just work.

After all, Ava and he were heading down the rural road toward the crash site. They'd have backup, or soon would anyway once Theo was on the way, but all of this could have been designed to kill Ava and him, especially if a lackey had been used to cause the crash with Caleb.

That would free up the killer to come after Ava.

Ava used her own phone to call Dispatch and request an ambulance, something Theo likely would have done, but this way the EMTs might make it there a little faster. Not as fast as Harley and her, though, not with the way he was speeding. He hit the sirens in case they did encounter any other traffic because Harley was very much afraid that every second counted right now.

"Caleb?" Ava called out when there was another moan. "Talk to me," she said. "Are you hurt?"

There were some other sounds. Not moans this time. But a soft swish followed by some quick movements. Harley tried to picture what was happening, and he had a bad thought flash in his head.

Oh, hell.

It sounded as if someone had thrown open the

door of Quentin's truck. If so, it probably hadn't been Quentin or Caleb since they would have had to bat down the airbags first.

"Caleb?" Ava repeated, her voice even louder this time.

But Caleb didn't answer. And the call disconnected.

When Harley glanced at her, he saw the alarm flash through her eyes and tried to tamp down his own worry. He wanted to reassure her that something could have been bumped to accidentally end the call, but there was no reassurance for this. Ava was almost certainly thinking the same thing he was.

That the killer had done this.

Her hands were trembling a little when she tried to call Quentin back. No answer and, after four rings, it went to voice mail. Ava didn't give up. She tried again, and when she got the same results, she tried Caleb's phone.

It rang and rang and rang. Each of the sounds feeling like a punch to the gut. It was possible that both phones had been damaged in the collision, or whatever the hell had happened, but it wasn't likely. And that brought him back full circle to something he had to accept.

That the killer had Quentin and Caleb.

"Check with Theo and see how far out he is," Harley instructed Ava, and he said a quick prayer that the sheriff wasn't that far behind them. He really didn't want to go into this with Ava without some kind of backup.

While she made that call, Harley continued to put the pedal to the metal and maneuver the cruiser around the snakelike road. The sun was setting, barely a sliver now on the horizon, and the darkness sure as heck wouldn't be their friend. They were going to arrive on scene in near darkness, where anything could be waiting for them.

"Theo just passed the Wilson Ranch," Ava relayed to him after she finished her call, and she immediately tried to contact Caleb again.

Harley mentally calculated the distance and silently cursed. If the crash had happened fifteen miles from Silver Creek, then Ava and he were less than three minutes away. Theo would be a good five minutes behind them.

After he arrived on scene, Harley hoped he would be able to talk Ava into staying in the cruiser while he checked on Caleb and Quentin. If necessary, he'd play dirty and remind her of the danger to the baby. He'd do whatever it took to keep her as safe as possible and hope that backup would arrive in time. While he was hoping, he added that the backup would be enough to stop whatever had been set in motion.

"Is Theo alone?" Harley asked her.

"Yes." Her strained voice indicated this was a big concern for her. "But he's called in a reserve deputy. He'll get here as fast as he can."

Well, that was better than nothing, and a reserve deputy would probably arrive a whole lot faster than he could get a Ranger out here. A Ranger who'd have to come all the way from the San Antonio office. He was considering having Ava call Grayson or someone else from the Silver Creek Ranch, but he rounded a steep curve and had to hit the brakes.

Just ahead, he spotted a black truck. Quentin's. It was off the road and in a deep ditch. The truck had tilted to the side with the passenger's-side door pressed against the ditch. The front end appeared to be damaged only at the impact point of the passenger's side hitting the ditch. The rear end was another story. It had been bashed in, and Harley could immediately see why.

Behind the truck was another vehicle. A massive Hummer, and judging from Harley's initial take of the scene, the Hummer had rear-ended the truck with enough force to send it into the ditch.

"I don't see Caleb," Ava muttered, though, like Harley, she was frantically looking around to spot Quentin, Caleb.

Or the killer.

But Harley didn't see anyone. Worse, the driver's-side door of the truck was shut, and he was almost positive he'd heard a vehicle door open.

Harley inched the cruiser forward, but he didn't bother to tell Ava to keep watch and be ready for an attack. She was. She had her gun gripped in her hand and had leaned in closer to the windshield.

He cut the sirens, hoping that would allow him to hear any sounds coming from outside. There was the spewing noise of a busted radiator on the Hummer, but that was it. Certainly, he couldn't hear any of those moans or anyone calling out for help.

Harley continued moving closer and stopped level with the truck. He kept the flashing cruiser lights on, though, to alert anyone who might be driving this way.

"I can't see through the truck's windows because of the heavy tint," Ava muttered.

Neither could he and he was thankful Ava hadn't gone into the panic mode and rushed out to check on Caleb.

Harley turned to her. "I'm less than two feet from the driver's door of the truck," he stated. "Just stay put a second and let me have a look inside. Please," he added when she opened her mouth, no doubt to argue. "I won't even fully get out of the cruiser. I'll just lower my window and reach over."

After a few seconds, she nodded, though she didn't look at all convinced this was a good idea. Still, like him, they had to know if Quentin or Caleb was all right.

Harley didn't waste any time. He lowered his window and, while muttering a quick prayer, he reached over to the truck, hoping that it didn't have an automatic locking system. If it did, Quentin had turned it off because Harley was able to open the door.

And he cursed.

Because it was empty.

Chapter Fifteen

The panic tore through Ava, threatening to bring her to her knees, but she fought it. Fought it hard because the panic wasn't going to help her find her son.

"Caleb?" she called out.

There was no need for her to stay silent. After all, the cruiser lights were flashing through the twilight, and if the killer was still there, he or she would know that Harley and she had arrived. Added to that, this had likely been the killer's plan all along; to use Caleb as bait and have them come here.

It had worked.

She refused to believe that Caleb or Quentin might already be dead. There'd be no reason for the killer to murder them right off the bat. Not when the two could be used to draw Harley and her out into the open.

"I don't see either of them," Ava observed as

she frantically glanced around her for any sign of them.

If they'd been hurt in the crash, they wouldn't have gotten far, but they were in an area of wide-open pastures and thick woods. Plenty of places for Quentin and Caleb to have run to escape a killer. Of course, that meant there were also plenty of places for the killer to lie in wait.

Harley leaned back inside the cruiser and, while he continued to keep watch, he tried to call Quentin. Ava listened for the sound of any ringing or vibrating, but she didn't hear anything to indicate the call had gone through.

She tried Caleb's number again and got the same thing. No response of any kind, and she seriously doubted that both Quentin's and Caleb's phone had become disabled in the crash.

"Theo should be about six to eight minutes out," Harley muttered, maybe calculating if they could wait that long.

Heaven knew what the killer was doing to Caleb right now, but Ava tried to keep that out of her mind and focus.

"Close your door and move up a little further," she advised. "Maybe they're in the pasture on the other side of the truck"

Harley had already started to do just that and, as he inched past the truck and Hummer, Ava looked on both sides of the road. On the road as well, since there could be explosives there. She didn't see anything.

Not until they were about ten feet past the Hummer.

"There," Harley and she said at the same time.

It was a man lying in a crumpled heap in the pasture. That gave her another slam of adrenaline and fear, but again, she forced herself to focus, and she released a quick breath when she saw the man move. She couldn't tell if it was Caleb or Quentin, but whoever it was, he appeared to be alive.

And injured.

Had to be since he wasn't getting up and wasn't in any kind of defensive posture to protect himself.

Harley turned the cruiser, switching to the high beams so they could get a better look. It was Quentin. Ava could now see his holster. No gun though. It was empty. And she could see something else.

Blood.

Harley must have seen it, too, because he cursed. It was on the side of Quentin's head and cheek. He'd either been injured in the crash or else the killer had done this to incapacitate him.

"Stay put and cover me," Harley insisted. "I have to go out there. I'll check the Hummer first and then get to Quentin."

Ava knew what Harley had to do. This was their job, and a fellow law enforcement officer needed their help. She also didn't want Harley to be gunned down, but she wouldn't be able to provide much cover if she stayed put.

"I'll get out and use my door as cover," she told him, making sure it didn't sound like a suggestion. "I can better cover you from over the roof of the cruiser."

She didn't add the reminder that she was wearing a bulletproof vest. So was Harley. But that wouldn't stop them from being killed with a headshot.

Harley hesitated. Of course he did. She was hesitating, too. But she met his gaze and tried to assure him that she would do everything possible to protect herself and their child.

"Don't leave the cover of the cruiser," he warned her and then stunned her by pressing a kiss to her mouth.

In the same motion, he barreled out of the cruiser, leaving his door open only a fraction. That way, it'd be easier for him to dive back in if trouble started, and the partially closed door would give her more protection.

Ava got out, too, and she took aim over the top of the cruiser. She silently repeated to herself that she was a good shot, and if she saw anyone coming after Harley and Quentin, she could stop them, especially since Harley was out in the open and at huge risk.

She focused on Harley as he threw open the door of the Hummer and looked inside. "Empty," he relayed to her, and he jumped over the ditch.

Ava kept her eyes on Harley, but she also couldn't stop listening for Caleb. If the killer had him, where would he take him? She had to guess that the killer had planned on using the Hummer to escape with Caleb, to take him someplace where he could hold him and use him to bargain.

And draw her out.

But with the Hummer disabled, the killer might not have had a choice but to flee with Caleb on foot. If so, then there'd be some kinds of signs like trampled grass or even footprints. There would have to be something they could use to find him and get him to safety. Ava couldn't allow herself to believe otherwise.

The cruiser lights created an eerie effect over the pasture. Not quite the jerky effect from strobe lights, but it made Harley's movements seem disjointed, as if every second he was hitting a pause button. And then there were the shadows. Too many of them all over the pasture and the woods.

It seemed to take an eternity for Harley to reach Quentin, but she figured it was only a couple of seconds. She saw Quentin move and then say something to Harley. Something that had Harley's head whipping in the direction of the woods that were straight ahead. Ava glanced there, too, but she didn't see anything.

"Quentin's been stunned," Harley called out to let her know. "And he has a head injury."

"Where's Caleb?" she immediately asked.

"Someone took him," Harley quickly supplied. "Quentin doesn't know who, but he thinks they went that direction." Harley pointed to the woods again, and that's when Ava saw the movement.

A flash of someone wearing light-colored clothing.

She didn't let it pull her complete attention from Harley since it could be a planned diversion. One that could turn out to be deadly. So she volleyed her gaze between Harley and the movement while she kept her gun ready in case she had to fire. Her heart slammed hard against her ribs when she caught sight of the person's face.

Caleb.

Her son was alive, and he was peering out from the trees as if hiding from someone.

Ava had to fight to stop herself from bolting from cover, and she yelled his name so he would know she was there. Something he likely already knew because of the lights. Caleb's head whipped up and he stepped out from the trees.

He didn't get far.

Someone latched onto him, dragging him

back. Ava got a glimpse of the gun the person rammed against Caleb's neck before they disappeared back into the woods.

HARLEY SAW WHAT had just happened to Caleb. While he'd knelt there next to Quentin, he'd seen Caleb's attacker drag him back into the cover of the trees. And, Harley cursed, because there was nothing he could do to stop it. He certainly hadn't been able to fire his gun since he couldn't risk hitting Caleb.

"Do what you have to do," Quentin muttered, his voice slurred from the effects of the stun gun. Maybe because of the head wound, too.

So far, Quentin hadn't been able to tell him what'd happened, but it looked as if someone had bashed him on the head. He needed an ambulance, and even though one was no doubt on the way, the EMTs wouldn't be able to move in unless the scene was secure.

"Go," Quentin insisted.

This was the very definition of a rock and a hard place. There wasn't anything else he could do for Quentin, but he could try to save Caleb. Of course, that meant going into the woods with a killer, but he couldn't just wait while Caleb was clearly in danger.

Obviously, Ava felt the same way, and Harley

had to curse again when he looked up and saw her making her way toward him.

"I have to help him," she said.

Harley didn't bother to spell out that this was exactly how the killer wanted her to react. No need. Ava knew the killer had set this plan in motion so she could end up being a victim.

He glanced at the woods, judging the distance, and it was about the same as it had been in Austin. The shooter had missed them with every single shot. Maybe the same thing would happen now.

"I'm a good cop," Ava added, no doubt to remind him that she wasn't just going to charge in with guns blazing.

Yeah, she was good, but Harley knew that sometimes good wasn't enough. Sometimes, the best cops got killed when trying to do the right thing.

"I'm going with you," Harley insisted.

He fired off a quick text to Theo to let him know what was happening, and then Harley started praying. First, that he could get Ava through this unharmed and then a prayer that they'd find Caleb alive and be able to take the killer into custody. Of course, that last part could be a long shot if Ava and he didn't manage to sneak up on the killer and take him or her by surprise. Hard to do, though, when the killer was no doubt keeping an eye on them.

"Backup weapon in my boot holster," Quentin managed to say.

Harley retrieved it for him, putting it into his hand. Since Quentin closed his fingers around it, the feeling was obviously returning, so at least he'd be able to defend himself if the killer circled back. Harley doubted that would happen though. If the killer had believed the Ranger would be a threat, then Quentin would already be dead.

"This way," Harley instructed. "And stay as low as you can."

He led Ava not toward the spot where they'd last seen Caleb. Instead, Harley made a beeline for the first cluster of trees. It was a huge risk. Anything was at this point. But it was better for them to have some cover, and then they could thread their way through the trees to get to Caleb.

If he was still there.

Harley had to believe he was. Though, it was entirely possible the killer'd had another vehicle waiting somewhere. Maybe up the road or on a nearby ranch trail. If that happened, if the killer managed to get Caleb out of these woods, then Harley figured Caleb's life wouldn't be worth much. The killer would likely use the young man as a bargaining tool and then murder him. After all, Quentin might not have gotten a good enough look to know the identity of the killer, but Caleb possibly would now that he'd had some up-close contact.

When Ava and he reached the cover of the trees, Harley didn't breathe any easier. Thankfully, there was a bright moon out, and his eyes had adjusted to the near darkness. He immediately looked around to see if they were about to be ambushed, since the killer could have anticipated they might do this. He didn't see anyone. Didn't hear anyone, either, but in the distance he could hear the sound of a siren. Theo, probably. That was good because they needed backup, and Theo would be able to decide if it was safe enough to allow in the EMTs to help Quentin.

Ava and he continued to move and Harley was once again thankful that she was in such good shape. He recalled her saying early on in the pregnancy that her doctor had told her that it was okay for her to keep up her exercise routine. This trek wouldn't necessarily be that strenuous, but the adrenaline and nerves had to be wreaking havoc with her head. Still, she kept up, moving fast with him as they made their way to where they would hopefully find Caleb.

Harley stopped when he thought he heard something. A footstep maybe. But it was hard to tell what with his heartbeat crashing in his ears. He forced himself to level out and listen, since he definitely didn't want the killer sneaking up on them and gunning them down.

Ava motioned toward their left, to an area even thicker with trees than where they already were. Apparently, she'd heard something, too, and like him, she was trying to pick through the darkness and the woods to see if there was a threat or if the sound they'd heard was just some animal trying to get out of their path.

They waited a few seconds. When there was nothing but the wail of the approaching siren, Ava and he started moving again. But they didn't get far. The next sound they heard sure as heck wasn't a footstep or an animal.

"Don't shoot," someone said. "It's me."

Harley cursed when he recognized that voice. Aaron.

The man stepped out from one of the trees, and he had his hands lifted in the air as if surrendering. Harley didn't let down his guard.

"Take aim at him," Harley told Ava. "I'll keep watch."

Ava did just that and was no doubt about to launch into some serious questions, but Aaron spoke first.

"What did you do with Caleb?" Aaron demanded. "Why the hell did you take him?"

It took Harley a moment to realize Aaron

meant that for Ava. Obviously, Aaron had gotten some things twisted up.

Or maybe this was all an act to make them think he was innocent.

But if he was the killer, if he'd been the one who'd taken his own son, then where was Caleb? Harley certainly didn't see him. It was possible, though, that Aaron had gagged him and stashed him behind one of the trees.

"I didn't take Caleb," Ava stated, her voice as cold as winter. "But if you did, you'd better tell me where he is now."

"I don't know where he is," Aaron insisted.

Ava kept her gun trained on him. "Then why are you out here?"

Aaron fluttered his hand toward the road. "I got a text from Caleb. He said he was in trouble and told me to come here."

"Right," Ava muttered, the skepticism coating that one word. Harley was right there with her. That wasn't likely to have happened.

Unless the killer had forced Caleb to send that text.

But Harley immediately discounted that. Unless Aaron had already been in Silver Creek, he wouldn't have been able to make it here ahead of Ava and him.

"It's true," Aaron argued. "I can show you the text."

"Texts can be faked," she argued right back. "This place isn't exactly on the beaten path. How could Caleb give you directions to get here?"

"He said I'd see a truck on the side of the road," Aaron answered without hesitation. He started to lower his arms, but Ava made a quick motion with the barrel of her gun for him to keep them in the air. "Caleb told me once I saw it that I was to park and wait. But then I saw you dragging him into the woods. What the hell happened, Ava? What's going on?"

If Aaron's story was anywhere near true, then the killer had to be the one who'd lured him here. But why? So Aaron could be killed, too, or was the killer looking to pin all of this on him? Of course, it was entirely possible that the story was all a pack of lies to get Ava and Harley to lower their guard so that Aaron could try to kill them.

Aaron huffed then he groaned. "I saw the truck on the road and the Hummer behind it. I saw the wreck. Was Caleb hurt? Tell me," he practically shouted when Ava didn't immediately respond.

"I don't know if Caleb is hurt, and I don't have him," she repeated. "Do you?"

She was no doubt looking for any signs that Aaron was lying. "You said you were parked just up the road?" Ava asked.

Harley cursed, and while he kept watch, he whipped out his phone to text Theo to let him know about the vehicle. He didn't want the killer using it to try to escape with Caleb.

"Yeah. Not far," Aaron verified. He groaned again. "What's going on?" This time his question was more like a plea. "Does the killer have Caleb?"

Before Ava could answer, Harley heard a sound coming from the area where they'd last seen Caleb. It was just a quick movement.

Then the bullet came right at them.

Chapter Sixteen

The bullet slammed into the tree just to Ava's right, less than a foot away. She automatically went to the ground, protecting her stomach, while she glanced over at Harley to make sure he was okay.

He was. For now anyway.

Like her, he dropped down, bringing up his gun to aim in the direction of where that shot had been fired. At first she thought it'd come from Aaron. But she could still see both of his hands, and Aaron didn't have a weapon.

"What the hell?" Aaron yelled.

He sounded genuinely shocked, but Ava knew that could be faked. Aaron could be calling the shots here, literally, since it could be his hired gun who'd just pulled the trigger.

A second shot came, this one blasting into the tree directly behind Harley and her. Aaron yelled out his question again, adding some vicious anger, and he went to the ground, scrambling to the side of the tree.

"Are the cops shooting at us?" Aaron shouted.

Ava didn't answer, but she knew it wasn't Theo or Quentin who was doing this. No way would either of them take that risk even if they had spotted Caleb with the killer. This wasn't a case of friendly fire. Just the opposite. These shots were coming from someone who wanted them dead.

"Ava?" somebody called out.

Her heart thudded when she realized it was Caleb. He was alive, but he sounded frantic. Of course he was. If he was close enough to the gunfire, this had to be terrifying for him.

She wanted to answer, but she knew she couldn't. Not when the killer might be using Caleb to try to pinpoint her exact location.

"Ava's here," Aaron shouted back. "I'm here, too. It's me… Aaron," he added, though she thought he'd been about to say *your dad*. "Where are you? We're worried sick about you."

The words had no sooner left Aaron's mouth when there were more shots. Three back-to-back blasts that tore through the woods, splintering the bark on the trees. Wood and leaves flew, and Ava sheltered her eyes and her stomach as best she could.

A sickening dread washed over her. Harley and she were in grave danger. That meant so was her precious baby. So was her son. She could lose everything right here, right now, without even knowing who was responsible for the hell they'd been going through.

So many dead women. So many ruined lives. And she still had no idea why the killer was after her.

"Aaron," Caleb responded, but this time his voice was different. Not so much frantic or terror but hesitation.

Ava tried not to think of what was being done to Caleb to make him call out to her. Maybe the killer was hurting him. Maybe killing him.

No, she couldn't go there. It would only cause her to lose focus, and she needed every bit of her attention and cop's training if they stood a chance of getting out of this alive.

"No," Caleb said, and he seemed to be arguing with someone.

If it was the killer in on that argument, then that might account for why there hadn't been any shots fired in the last couple of seconds. Then again, it could be a ploy by the killer to draw them out, to make them believe they wouldn't be gunned down.

"Keep watch," Harley murmured to her.

He touched her arm, just a touch, but that was enough to help steady her. Well, steady her until she realized Harley was on the move. He stayed hunkered down, but he left the cover of the tree and darted to another one. Then another. He was making his way in the direction of where they'd heard Caleb.

Mercy, Harley had to stay safe. He had to come back to her. This didn't have anything to do with them having had sex. No, this was about her feelings for him. She was still in love with him and she needed the chance to tell him that.

"Caleb?" Aaron called out again. He groaned when Caleb didn't respond.

Ava silently had a much worse reaction. Terror for her son. But she continued watching, looking for the killer. She also kept an eye on Aaron, wishing that she could just frisk him to make sure he wasn't armed. He hadn't turned his back to her once so, for all she knew, he could have a gun in the waist of his jeans. He could be waiting for the perfect moment to kill her.

But if that was so, it meant he wasn't working alone.

With the explosives expert almost certainly dead, it was possible that Aaron had hired some muscle to carry out this sick plan.

"The person with Caleb had your face," Aaron muttered. "I thought it was you. I thought you'd lost it and wanted him out of the way."

Her face. That would certainly mesh with how the killer had staged his other victims. A mask of her face to carry out all those murders. And now this. The killer was using her face while doing heaven knew what to her son. Caleb would know it wasn't her, but that likely wouldn't be of much comfort now.

She thought of the other two suspects. Marnie and Duran. Thought of her father, too. If Aaron had been duped into coming here, then it was likely one of them was behind this. Not her father though. He wouldn't have dirtied his hands this way, but Duran, yes, he could absolutely be the one who'd grabbed Caleb and pulled him into the woods. Marnie, too. One of them could be out there right now, waiting to put the finishing touches on this plan of terror.

A gunshot blast cut off those thoughts and had Ava's heart dropping. *Please no, not Harley or Caleb*. She pivoted in the direction of the sound but didn't hear anything to indicate one of them had been hurt. No sharp sounds of pain, no one dropping to the ground.

She could no longer see Harley, but she believed she could hear his footsteps about fifteen yards away. Maybe he was moving so he could then circle back to Caleb and whoever was holding him. Or the footsteps could belong to the killer. If so, he didn't appear to be dragging anyone in tow. So, if that was indeed what was happening, then where was Caleb?

Since Quentin had been hit with a stun gun, the killer might not have hesitated to use it on Caleb. That would be especially true if Caleb was fighting to get free. Added to that, it hadn't worked to lure her out when Caleb had shouted for her, so the killer might have just stashed him somewhere to use her for another ploy.

"Caleb?" Aaron repeated, his voice a weak sob now.

Ava ignored the man so she could focus on Harley and the direction he was going. Even though he was no longer close to her, she could maybe still give him some kind of backup. She had to keep watch for Theo, too. It would take him a while to get out of the cruiser and then deal with Quentin, but after that, the sheriff would no doubt be making his way toward them.

Another shot came at them.

But not at her.

Ava quickly realized that when she heard Aaron howl in pain. Her gaze fired over to him and she saw that he'd been shot in his right shoulder. The blood immediately started to spread over his shirt. Not gushing, but this didn't appear to be just a graze or a flesh wound either.

Writhing in pain, Aaron fell all the way to the ground, clutching his shoulder. In all his moving around, Ava got a good look at the back of his jeans and didn't see any weapons. Then again, she doubted now that he was truly the killer unless his own henchman had shot him by mistake.

"An ambulance will be here soon," she muttered to him. Though Ava had no idea when that would happen with the gunshots being fired all around them. "Keep pressure on the wound until help gets here," she added.

Even though Aaron wasn't her priority—Caleb and Harley were—she still didn't want him to bleed out. It was possible Aaron was innocent of everything that'd happened, and even if he had actually had some part in it, Ava wanted him alive so he could fill them in on any details he might know. She wanted any and all info that could catch this killer and end the murders.

Her head whipped up when she heard the sound of running footsteps. They definitely weren't coming from the area where Harley should be. No, these were in the area where those shots had originated, and that meant the shooter was on the move. Maybe trying to escape. Maybe trying to go after Harley or Caleb.

She heard something else. Something that had every muscle tightening in Ava's body. A moan, the sound of someone in pain. She couldn't stay put, not after hearing that, and she wasn't much good to Harley or Caleb if she didn't at least try to help.

Ava bolted away from the tree and went after the killer.

HARLEY KEPT MOVING, kept looking for any signs of Caleb and the person who'd grabbed him. It was next to impossible to see drag marks, footprints or such, but he had heard something that gave him a good idea of the killer's movements.

Movements that could have gotten Ava killed.

He refused to dwell on that because just the thought of it twisted him up inside. Instead, Harley focused on doing whatever he could to put a quick end to this so he could rescue Caleb and then hurry back to Ava.

Harley had no doubts that the killer or someone working for the killer had gone to the area where he'd left Ava and Aaron. He'd had no trouble hearing the shots. Had no trouble imagining what those bullets could be doing. That's why Harley had backtracked and headed that direction, to try to take out the shooter before he or she could do any more damage.

But then the snake had gone on the move again.

Not slow, cautious steps, either, but moving fast. Harley was pretty sure the person was heading back to the original spot where Ava and he had first seen Caleb being grabbed.

Harley didn't make a beeline in that direction. That would be too dangerous, to come at the killer head-on, so he went back to his original plan of circling around to hopefully come up from the side. That'd be his best bet for getting a clean shot to stop whatever the hell was happening right now.

He tried to avoid stepping on any fallen tree branches so he wouldn't telegraph his movements, but he was certain he was making plenty of noise. That wouldn't help with the element of surprise. However, the killer had to know that Ava and he would be doing everything possible to get Caleb out of there safely.

That would mean a confrontation with the killer.

Harley welcomed it. Welcomed the chance to stop the killer from doing any more harm. But he was going to have to make sure the SOB didn't get the chance to stop him first.

He paused when he heard yet more footsteps. Close ones. Not running ones this time, and they were getting closer to him. He held his breath, listening and waiting. Then he had to curse when he caught some movement from the corner of his eye and realized it wasn't the killer or Caleb.

It was Ava.

Harley was beyond thankful that she didn't appear to be hurt, but he wanted to demand to know what the hell she was doing there. He didn't have to wait long, though, for her to tell him.

"The shooter's moving that way," she whispered, tipping her head further to the left than he'd been heading.

If he'd continued on his path, he might have ended up having a face-to-face instead of sneaking up on him or her.

"Aaron's been shot," Ava added before Harley could wonder how she'd known that. "The shooter fired and then went in that direction." She motioned to his left again, and then her eyes met his. "I couldn't stay put."

Yeah, he'd already figured that out. In some ways, it was easier having her with him because he didn't have to imagine what terrible things might have been happening to her. But having her there was also a distraction, because Harley would do anything to protect her.

Anything.

"How bad is Aaron hurt?" Harley asked.

"A bullet to the shoulder," she supplied.

So that meant Aaron was likely out of commission. Well, unless he'd faked his injury, and Harley wouldn't put it past the man to do something like that. But if Aaron was truly injured, it meant Ava and he were about to face either

Duran or Marnie. Of course, it could also be someone they'd hired. More than one, in fact.

If so, that meant Ava and he could be walking into a trap.

Harley had silenced his phone, but he felt it vibrate, and he took it out so he could glance at the screen. "It's Theo," he relayed to Ava. "He's heading into the woods now."

Keeping watch while trying to listen to their surroundings, Harley fired off a quick text to let Theo know about Aaron being shot and to give the sheriff a general idea of where they were. Hard to do that, though, when Harley wasn't sure. However, Theo would have heard the gunshots and would have an idea of where to go.

Harley put away his phone and turned to Ava, to remind her to stay behind him and let him shield her. But he already knew she would be as cautious as she possibly could be. So that's why he just settled for dropping a quick kiss on her mouth and got them moving.

He didn't move with a barreling pace, and that wasn't all for Ava's benefit. Harley wanted to be able to hear any little sound despite them trudging through the thick underbrush and weaving around the trees.

And he finally heard something.

Movement in the area right where Ava had pointed out. Harley didn't head straight there.

Going with his plan of circling around, he went even further to the left, almost in a straight line while he kept watch from the corner of his eye for any glimpse of Caleb or his captor.

Each step felt like a huge risk, knowing Ava and he could be shot. But he was beyond thankful when no bullets came at them.

Harley stopped when he finally saw something. Ava must have spotted it at the same time because she quit moving and turned in the direction of a small clearing. Emphasis on *small*. There was only about a ten-foot strip where there were no trees, and the moonlight filtered in enough for Harley to see someone.

Caleb.

He was alive, and Harley knew the breath Ava dragged in was one of relief.

At first glance, it appeared that Caleb was alone and leaning against one of the trees on the far perimeter of the clearing. Maybe placed there as human bait to get Ava and him to go rushing in after the young man. But then Harley saw the gun and realized that someone dressed all in black was behind Caleb and pressing the barrel to his head.

Ava's next breath definitely wasn't one of relief because she knew her son could end up being killed right in front of her.

Harley tried to make out anything about the

person who was holding Caleb, but it was hard to do since they had hunkered down, using Caleb as a shield. That would prevent Harley or Ava from trying a head shot. Or anywhere else for that matter since they could end up shooting Caleb.

"I'm supposed to tell you something," Caleb said, his voice trembling. "A trade. Me for you, Ava. But I don't want you to do that," he blurted out.

The person holding him acted fast by ramming the barrel of the gun against his temple and tightening the chokehold around his neck.

Of course, it had come down to this. It was always about getting to Ava, and the killer knew she would want to save her son. But Caleb wasn't her only child. The daughter she was carrying had to be protected, too.

"I'll offer a trade," Harley stated, not to Caleb or Ava. But to the killer. "Me for Caleb."

Harley couldn't hear the killer's response but, judging from the way Caleb flinched, he'd just been given a reply to pass along.

"No deal." Caleb let him know and then he paused. "If I'm dead, I can't be used to—"

That was as far as Caleb got before his captor bashed the gun against his head again. This time, it drew blood that began to slide down the side of Caleb's face.

Because Ava's arm was against his, Harley

sensed her tense and could practically feel the anger coming off her. It was torture watching this being done to her child.

"No, I won't," Caleb snarled, and this time, Harley was certain he was talking to the killer.

Caleb moved as if to try to break free of the chokehold, but the killer hung on. In the shuffle, though, the killer also moved. Not much. Just enough for a shot. It wouldn't be a kill shot to the head but rather to the killer's right leg that was now extended out from Caleb's body.

"I've got this," Ava muttered.

She didn't waste a second. With her hand steady, Ava took aim and fired.

AVA KNEW THIS wasn't a shot she could miss, but it was still a risk.

A huge one.

After all, she couldn't put the bullet in the killer's head so he or she could just reflexively pull the trigger and kill Caleb on the spot. Still, this was the best chance they had of getting all of them out of there alive, especially since there was no way the killer would let Caleb live even if Ava did sacrifice herself for him.

The shot sliced into the killer's leg and Ava immediately heard the cry of pain. Not a man's voice. No. A woman's.

Marnie's.

Caleb took advantage of the injury by diving to the ground. Or rather, trying to do that, but Marnie just dropped down with him, pulling him back into the chokehold and putting her gun to his head.

"You want him to die?" Marnie shouted, the pain and desperation coating her voice. Both were lethal factors here since they could lead Marnie to do something that almost certainly wasn't part of her original plan.

The woman could make sure all four of them died right here, right now.

Ava tried not to look at Caleb. Hard to do, though, but if she focused on him, it would be a huge mistake. She had to push all thoughts of him aside and try to treat this like any other hostage situation.

Marnie leaned her head out just a fraction from Caleb's, and Ava kept her gun trained on her as Marnie ripped off her mask. Something inside Ava unclenched. The situation was still as dangerous as it got, but it sickened her that Marnie was doing all of this while wearing the image of Ava's face.

"It wasn't supposed to be like this," Marnie said, groaning in pain and cursing. "I should be gone now in the Hummer."

"Gone with Caleb?" Ava asked. She stayed behind the cover of the tree but kept watch for any chance of a clean shot. Beside her, Harley was no doubt doing the same thing.

"Of course gone with Caleb. I shouldn't have to be crawling around in the woods. You weren't supposed to die here. I wanted that to happen in front of Aaron. Where is the SOB? Did I kill him?"

Ava debated how to respond. She wanted Marnie to keep talking, but if the woman found out Aaron had only been injured and wasn't dead, that might cause her to start shooting again.

"I'm not sure if Aaron is still alive," Ava settled for saying. "He was bleeding out when I left him."

"Good," Marnie spat out. "I hope he dies a slow, painful death, and if there's any life in his worthless body when I find him, I'll show him pictures of his dead son and his ex-lover. I'll kill you both and show him what I've done."

Ava had already guessed all of this was to get back at Aaron. Marnie obviously hated the man.

"Aaron has to pay for killing my sister," Marnie went on, and this time her wail turned into a sob.

The woman was quickly losing control of herself. Again, not good. Because it would be impossible to bargain with a woman who felt she had nothing else to lose.

Harley didn't say anything, but he moved away from her, heading toward the other side of the clearing so he could no doubt try to come up from behind Marnie. Ava covered his movement by shifting her body just enough to step on some twigs and leaves beneath her boots. The sound might not fool Marnie, so Ava went with what she hoped would be a distraction.

"Your plan was organized," Ava said, making sure to sound like a cop. "Until tonight, we had no idea you were the one who murdered those women."

"Of course it was organized," Marnie snapped, groaning again. "I worked hard on the details, and it shouldn't have come down to this. You should be dead, and I shouldn't be bleeding. Hell, this hurts. I should hurt your son to make you pay."

That felt as if Marnie had punched her. There was nothing else the woman could have said to give her that jolt of fear. Oh, mercy. Her son could die.

"Caleb didn't do anything to Christina," Ava tried, hoping to give Harley time to get to Marnie. "That was all on Aaron. He gave her the drugs, didn't he?"

"Yes. He killed my beautiful baby sister." That caused Marnie to start crying. "He killed her, and I had to pretend to be friendly with him. Every time I saw him, I wanted to shoot him in the face, but that would have been too easy. I wanted him to pay."

"And then you were going to set him up for the murders," Ava finished for her.

"Oh, yeah. I chose women who'd been pregnant. I figured that'd convince the cops that Aaron's targets were to get back at you. And then he would have been arrested, convicted and paid and paid and paid by being locked up in a maximum-security prison where the inmates could make his life a living hell."

Ava didn't spell out to Marnie that her plan had also made others' lives a living hell. There were four dead women, and their families were dealing with the pain and grief Marnie had caused. In that moment, Ava wished Marnie as much pain and misery as she'd planned for Aaron.

Ava finally spotted Harley, but her chest muscles were too tight for her to feel any kind of relief. He was only about ten yards behind Marnie and Caleb, and he was inching his way toward them.

"You killed your explosives expert." Ava threw it out there. She purposely raised her voice to try to cover the sound of Harley's footsteps.

"The fool," Marnie spat out. "I hired him, and then he tried to milk more money from me. He had no idea who he was dealing with."

No, he hadn't, and it'd been a costly mistake. Marnie was capable of anything, and that was especially unsettling since she still had the gun aimed at Caleb's head.

"And I'm guessing you chose the women to kill because you knew they wouldn't put up much of a fight," Ava said, knowing that wouldn't be true.

"I'm not a coward," Marnie practically yelled. "I

chose them because they were connected to you. So that the fool cops would think Aaron killed them so he could get revenge on your father."

Yes, Ava had figured that out. And it sickened her to think that it might have worked.

Since Harley would be closing in on Marnie soon, Ava went with what she hoped would be a step closer to saving Caleb's life. She made eye contact with him and then sharply cut her glance to the ground to his left. She waited, praying that Caleb understood. He did. He gave her a slight nod.

Caleb's movement caused Marnie to tighten the chokehold, but he was still able to move. He jerked to the left.

Just as Ava stepped out from the tree.

A distraction to get Marnie's attention on her. It worked. The woman's gaze whipped toward her. So did Marnie's gun. Just as Ava darted back behind the tree.

Marnie fired.

So did Harley.

Both shots seemed to blast through the woods at the same exact second. Marnie's bullet missed, smacking into the tree right next to Ava. Harley's didn't miss. His shot went straight into Marnie's head. The woman made a sharp, strangled gasp. And then slumped to the side.

Dead.

Chapter Seventeen

Harley focused on Ava. Just Ava. With the adrenaline still slamming through him, it was next to impossible to process the details of what had just happened, so he grasped onto the most important thing.

And that was Ava.

He didn't respond to the texts he was getting. No doubt updates from anyone who was now on scene in the woods where Ava and he had been lured. He'd deal with the updates and the aftermath of the investigation later, but for now, he watched as the doctor pressed the little stethoscope wand to Ava's stomach. And Harley prayed that the baby was all right.

Ava was covered in nicks and bruises that she'd gotten when they'd made their frantic hunt through the woods so they could get to Caleb. None of her injuries looked serious, and she had insisted that she hadn't fallen or been bumped on her stomach, but she hadn't protested the trip to the Silver Creek emergency room to make sure all truly was well.

Harley felt his own cuts and bruises. All minor stuff. It was the same for Caleb, though he was undergoing his own exam in the room next door. They'd gotten damn lucky that none of them had been shot or killed.

Marnie had definitely gotten the worst of it.

And she'd deserved it.

Harley never took it lightly when he discharged his weapon, but it had been a life-and-death matter with Marnie. The woman had been hell-bent on killing to avenge her sister, and she hadn't cared one bit that she'd harmed and murdered so many innocent people. He figured there was a special place in hell for a person who'd done something like that.

"The baby's heartbeat is good," Dr. Medina said, causing both Ava and Harley to blow out breaths of relief. "There's not a scratch on your stomach," he added to Ava. "And, despite everything, your vitals are good."

Harley got another wave of relief that unclenched some of the muscles in his chest and stomach. It was somewhat of a miracle that Ava had managed to come out of this unscathed. Well, physically anyway. He knew there'd be plenty of emotional stuff for her to deal with, and he could curse Marnie for giving Ava what would likely be nightmares for life.

"How are you feeling?" the doctor asked Ava.

She opened her mouth, probably to give a rote response of "fine," but then she drew in a breath as long as the one she'd released. "I'll be a whole lot better now that the killer is dead and after I find out if Caleb is okay."

Dr. Medina gave her a gentle pat on the back. What the doctor didn't do was ask why she was so worried about Caleb, which meant he might have already heard some buzz about Ava being the young man's mother. That buzz could have easily started when the ambulance had arrived on scene and Ava had muttered for them to see to "her son." Harley hadn't even been sure that she'd known she had said it since he figured she'd been dealing with the shock of what had just happened.

"Doctor Jenkins is with Caleb now," Medina said. "I'm sure he'll be finished soon, and then you'll be able to speak to him." The doctor shifted his attention to Harley. "Now that we know Ava and your baby are all right, why don't I have a look at you?"

Harley shook his head. He wasn't sure he could stave off the adrenaline long enough to sit for an exam. Plus, it wasn't necessary. "Nothing hurts," he settled for saying.

That wasn't a lie. Harley couldn't feel anything but the slight sting from his very minor injuries. It wasn't enough to waste time with an exam, especially since he wanted to focus on Ava.

"Suit yourself," the doctor muttered, standing from the exam stool where he'd been sitting. He gave Ava another pat. "Go home, get some rest. Let Harley give you a little TLC."

Harley wondered if there'd been buzz, too, about Ava and him. Probably. Everyone would have known he'd been staying at her house during the hunt for the killer. Added to that, the doctor could probably sense the connection between them. A connection that went beyond the baby she was carrying.

Diving right into some of the TLC, Harley took hold of Ava's arm to help her off the exam table, and she looked at him. "You've been getting a lot of texts since you've been in here with me."

"Texts that can wait," he assured her, and even though the doctor was still there, Harley slipped his arm around her waist, easing her to him, and he kissed her.

Man, he needed that. Needed to hold her and have her mouth on his. It couldn't last, of course. This wasn't the time or the place for a heated kissing session, but he'd wanted her to know he was there for her in any and all ways.

She gave him a slight smile when she eased back, and while some of the worry in her eyes had faded, there was still plenty there. That wouldn't be going away until she knew Caleb's status.

The doctor smiled, too, doled out a goodbye and headed out of the exam room. So did Ava and Harley. He kept his arm around her waist, and not only did Ava not move away from it, she also adjusted her body so she was even closer to him.

When they stepped into the waiting area, Harley was glad to see that only Theo was there, and he was reading something on his phone. Harley had thought that maybe there'd be a few gawkers or gossip hunters around, but thankfully folks had stayed away.

"Everything okay?" Theo immediately asked Ava.

She nodded and looked at the other exam room where Caleb was. The door was still closed.

"No word on Caleb yet," Theo let her know. "But I just got an update on Aaron. He's in surgery, but the initial report is that his injury isn't life-threatening."

That was good, especially since Marnie's confession made it obvious that Aaron hadn't had any involvement in the murders. "Did Aaron say anything about Marnie when he was in the ambulance?"

Not that there would have been much for the man to say, but Harley knew that Deputy Nelline Rucker had ridden in the ambulance with Aaron. Nelline would have reported anything back to Theo.

"Nelline informed Aaron that Marnie was the killer," Theo explained. "Aaron filled in the blanks, and I think it hit him pretty hard just how close Marnie came to succeeding in setting him up for the murders. Apparently, Aaron seemed grateful that she'd failed rather than gripe about us having him on the suspect list."

Harley wouldn't have cared a rat about the griping. There'd been probable cause for them to believe Aaron might be guilty. And the man was likely guilty of supplying those drugs to Christina and withholding that he'd been the one responsible. Aaron would no doubt end up paying for that, maybe even with some jail time, depending on whether or not the local DA would want to pursue it.

"What about Quentin?" Harley asked. There was probably something about that on his phone, but he didn't want to let go of Ava so he could check.

"He's fine," Theo assured him. "Once the effects of the stun gun wore off, he decided to stay at the crime scene to assist the deputies and the CSIs." He looked at Ava. "He was cursing himself, though, for not stopping Marnie when she threw open his door after ramming the Hummer into his truck. He was apparently a little disoriented, and he saw the mask Marnie was wearing."

Yeah, a mask of Ava's face. There was no way Quentin would have just fired if he'd thought it was Ava. Of course, after a split second or two, the Ranger would have realized it was a mask, but by then it would have been too late. Marnie would have hit him with the stun gun and then taken Caleb.

"Did Quentin happen to say how he made it out of the truck and into the pasture?" Ava pressed. Harley had wondered the same thing, though Quentin hadn't gone far from the collision.

"He said he crawled there after he got back some of the feeling in his legs, but then he collapsed. He was trying to go after Marnie and Caleb."

"I'm surprised Marnie didn't just kill him," Harley commented.

"Quentin was surprised, too, but I guess that wasn't part of her plan," Theo said. "Of course, judging from what you and Ava told me, it hadn't been part of Marnie's plan for the crash to disable the Hummer."

True, the woman had obviously planned on

using it to escape with Caleb and then use Caleb to draw out Ava. With Aaron already on scene, he would have looked guilty. On the surface anyway. But the CSIs would have examined Quentin's truck and known that Aaron's vehicle hadn't been responsible. Marnie had likely planned a fix for that, but it was a detail they might never learn since the woman hadn't been able to carry out the finale of her sick plan.

The doors to the ER slid open and all three of them turned in that direction. Harley automatically put his hand over his gun, proof that he was still battling the adrenaline. He got another slight surge of it when he saw the two men who came rushing in.

Edgar and Duran.

Great. Just what Ava didn't need on top of everything else, and Harley geared up for his usual sparring battle with the senator. At least he now knew that Duran wasn't a killer. That didn't mean, though, that he still couldn't be a thorn in Ava's side.

"Ava," Edgar said the moment he spotted her.

Edgar made a beeline toward her, and for a moment, Harley thought the man was about to pull her into his arms. He stopped just short of her, no doubt recalling that Ava wouldn't want such a gesture from him.

"I'm not hurt," Ava said right off.

Edgar slid glances at both Harley and her, silently questioning if that was true when he obviously noticed the nicks and bruises. "Good," Edgar murmured, sounding both genuine and relived. "And Caleb?"

Ava's body tensed. "Still waiting to hear. He's in the exam room."

Edgar nodded but didn't jump to say anything. Maybe because he didn't know what he could say, considering he'd forced Ava to give up Caleb all those years ago.

"I'm hearing reports that all of this is connected to Aaron," her father said.

"All of this is connected to Marnie Dunbar," Ava corrected. "She confessed to the murders and planned to set up Aaron."

Harley glanced at Duran, expecting the man to balk about having ever been a suspect. He didn't. Maybe, like Aaron, he was just thankful he was alive and the danger was over.

Of course, things still weren't resolved on several levels.

Not with Ava and Caleb. Not with her and her father. Not with Harley. But Harley was hoping to work on that once he was able to get Ava to himself.

Edgar's attention landed on the arm Harley still had around Ava, and while his mouth didn't exactly turn into a scowl, there was the initial punch of disapproval. Much to Harley's surprise, however, that faded.

"If you had any part in keeping Ava safe," Edgar said, "then thank you."

Harley shrugged and figured that was as close to a compliment as he'd ever get from the man.

Edgar went silent again, but it was obvious there were things he wanted to say. Maybe to try to start resolving things between Ava and him. The man must have decided that was a lost cause, though, because he muttered a goodbye and turned as if to leave. He didn't get far. Edgar immediately turned back around.

"I'm sorry," he blurted. "For a lot of things." He added a glance to Harley, maybe to let him know that part of the blanket apology was for him. Edgar swallowed hard. "I'd like to see my granddaughter when she's born. If that's possible," he tacked on.

Ava took her time answering. Several long moments crawled by. "All right," she finally said. "But only if you show due respect to Harley. He is her father."

Edgar nodded, and even though Harley figured the man would have some trouble with that respect thing, he still saw this as a start in the right direction. Ava didn't need Edgar to be part of her life. Their daughter wouldn't, either, but a grandparent was good for a child to have. Added to that, it could perhaps end up mending some of the old wounds between Ava and him.

"Goodbye," Edgar muttered, but it didn't have his usual impatient snarl to it. "Keep them safe," he added to Harley.

Edgar and Duran again seemed to be on the verge of walking away, but the exam room door opened and Caleb came out. He stopped when he spotted them, giving each a glance, maybe to see if there'd been some kind of argument in progress. Obviously, he didn't see signs of that and started toward them.

"Are you okay?" Ava asked, directing her question both at Caleb and the doctor who stayed in the exam room door. The doctor gave her a thumbs-up.

"I'm fine," Caleb assured her. "How about you and Harley?"

They both echoed Caleb's response, but Ava placed her hand on Caleb's jaw, turning him so she could do her own exam. Like them, Caleb had his share of small cuts, and the bruise on his head from where Marnie had hit him with the gun, but it didn't look that serious. Harley was glad to see that someone had cleaned the blood off his neck and face. Not Caleb's, but rather the spatter from Marnie's head wound.

"Thank you," Caleb said, also extending his

appreciation to both of them. "Trust me, I'm very thankful you're both good shots."

Harley was thankful for that, too. Both Ava and he had put bullets in a killer, and they'd had only small windows for those shots.

"Sir," Caleb greeted Edgar when he finally turned his attention to the man. He nodded an acknowledgment to Duran as well. There was no anger in Caleb's expression or tone, though he had to know by now the part Edgar and Duran had played in his being put up for adoption.

"Caleb," Edgar said back. "I was just telling Ava that I hoped I'd be able to see my granddaughter when she's born." He paused, cleared his throat. "Maybe you'll be there for that so I can see both of you."

Caleb looked at Ava, no doubt to get her take, and when she only nodded, Caleb smiled. "Sounds good."

That seemed to cause Edgar to relax a little and he offered Caleb his hand. Caleb shook it, and then Duran and Edgar left with Duran already muttering something about Edgar needing to schedule a press conference.

Caleb's phone dinged with a text and he glanced down at the screen. "That's Quentin. He's out front in a borrowed cruiser and said he'd give me a lift home. Is it all right if I go?" he asked Theo.

"Sure. You can give your statement tomorrow morning. If you can't come here for that, I can send Ava and Harley to Austin to take it."

Caleb smiled again. "Either way is fine. Call me and let me know what works best for you," he told Harley and Ava.

"One more thing," Ava said when Caleb started to leave. "The press will soon pick up on you being my son. There could be reporters."

Caleb made a dismissive sound. "I'll handle it," he assured her, and then the young man did something that had Harley silently cheering. Caleb hugged Ava. "See you tomorrow," he added in a whisper, and his smile widened when she brushed a kiss on his cheek.

Apparently, that was another part of Ava's life— a huge one—that just might have a happy resolution. Of course, they'd need to keep an eye on Caleb, and it was possible he'd require counseling for what he'd gone through. If so, they'd make sure he got it and anything else he needed. Caleb wasn't his bio-son, but he was a brother to Harley's daughter, and that made him kin in Harley's book.

Caleb walked toward the exit and turned back to wave at them. "I love you," Ava blurted out to him, causing Caleb to flash her an even bigger smile.

"Love you, too," Caleb said. He was still smiling as he walked out the door.

The tears immediately sprang to Ava's eyes. Happy ones. But she quickly wiped them away. No way would she want her boss to see her crying.

"I'll go have a word with Quentin," Theo muttered. "To see if he has any updates from the CSIs."

That was a ploy on Theo's part to give them some time alone, since Quentin would have already texted any updates before he'd left those woods. Harley was glad, though, that Theo had played the ploy card because he really did want time alone with Ava.

Since the ER wasn't exactly a private place, Harley took Ava by the hand and led her back into the exam room. He shut the door and pulled her into his arms. She practically melted against him, and he steeled himself in case she broke down into a full sob.

But she didn't.

When she looked up at him, he saw that her eyes were still a little misty with tears, but she didn't look anywhere on the verge of sobbing.

"Our lives have changed so much in the past forty-eight hours," she murmured.

Yeah, they had, and if Harley had his way, there'd be other changes. Good ones, he hoped. He'd intended to kiss Ava again, to get those good changes started, but she beat him to it. She slipped her arms around his neck, pulled him to her and kissed him as if there were no tomorrow.

Or better yet—as if there were plenty of tomorrows.

Mindful of her injuries, Harley tried to keep the kiss gentle, but Ava apparently wanted to go in an entirely different direction. Her mouth was hungry and hot, filled with so much need. And it released the ball of tension inside him, since that need was for him.

He kissed her back, going hungry and hot as well, until he robbed both of them of their breaths. They stopped only for some much-needed oxygen and dived right back in for a second kiss. This one fueled the heat, but it also settled the rest of their raw nerves. A good solid attraction could do that.

Love could do it even faster.

Harley probably could have chosen a better time, a better place than an exam room in the ER, but he didn't want to wait another second. He wanted the whole package with Ava, and he needed her to hear that now. Better yet, he needed her to want the same thing he did.

"I'm in love with you," he said when the second kiss broke. He stayed close to her, his forehead pressed against hers while they stayed body to body and breath to breath.

Harley waited. And waited. That tension started to coil inside him again when Ava didn't immediately respond, but then he realized she wasn't talking because she was gathering enough air so that she could speak.

"Good," she finally said. "Because I'm in love with you, too. I was worried about how you'd react when I told you."

"Worried?" He eased back now so he could meet her gaze.

She nodded. "I wasn't sure you were ready for it."

The tension vanished and Harley smiled. "Ava, I've never been more ready for anything in my entire life." He slid his hand between them and over her stomach.

Over their baby.

Oh, yeah, this life, this love, was exactly what Harley wanted.

* * * * *

*Look for the previous books in
USA TODAY bestselling author
Delores Fossen's miniseries,
Silver Creek Lawmen: Second Generation:*

Targeted in Silver Creek
Maverick Detective Dad
Last Seen in Silver Creek

*Available now wherever Harlequin Intrigue
books are sold*

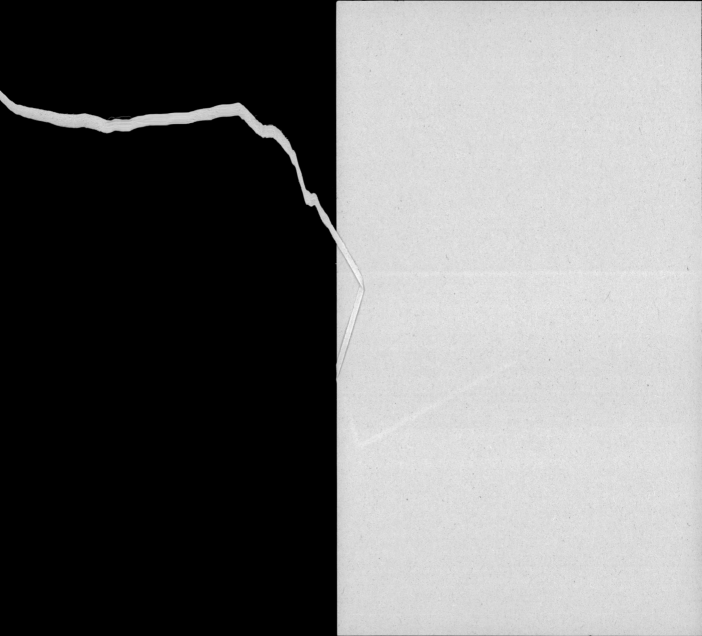